The
Veneration
of
Monsters

Also by Suzanne Burns

Misfits and Other Heroes

The
Veneration
of
Monsters

//

Suzanne Burns

DZANC
BOOKS

5220 Dexter Ann Arbor Rd.
Ann Arbor, MI 48103
www.dzancbooks.org

First US edition: July 2017

ISBN: 978-1-941088-76-0

Book design by Steven Seighman

Library of Congress Cataloging-in-Publication Data

Names: Burns, Suzanne, 1973- author. Title: The veneration of monsters
: stories / Suzanne Burns. Description: Ann Arbor, MI : Dzanc Books,
2017. Identifiers: LCCN 2016038925 (print) | LCCN 2016044728 (eb-
ook) | ISBN   9781941088760 (paperback) | ISBN 9781945814112 ()
Subjects: | BISAC: FICTION / Short Stories (single author). | FIC-
TION /   Literary. Classification: LCC PS3602.U767 A6 2017 (print) |
LCC PS3602.U767 (ebook) | DDC 813/.6--dc23LC record available
at https://lccn.loc.gov/2016038925

Printed in the United States of America

10   9   8   7   6   5   4   3   2   1

In loving memory
of Kelly John O'Ryan

Brother
Friend
Renaissance Man

Contents

First Movement

For Shirley Jackson

Cherise wanted to meet a man who would call her mouth a symphony. Not because of all the things she had learned to do with her lips, the precise way she blotted her lipstick with a cloth napkin at fine restaurants, how she pouted to win arguments without anyone catching on, her suitors and debaters unaware Cherise had snared them in a series of charming little traps.

Her lips even helped form her infamous bubble laugh, recognizable as she thumbed through tabloids at a grocery store or watched the slapdash flicker of previews before any feature film, usually by herself. Cherise's lips had helped her land first dates and jobs at perfume counters and the biggest piece of cake at birthday parties, but none of this ever lasted, or in any way evoked a symphony. Cherise was ready for her overture to begin.

Single for more years than not, at thirty-six Cherise wanted to become a different woman, but not from plastic surgery, dieting, or even bleaching her hair. Cherise vowed to recreate herself by becoming unique. She loved how unique the word "unique" sounded as she made room on her small bathroom counter for her coffee cup among a tower of half-used makeup containers that perpetually smeared her fingertips.

Cherise stared at her lips in the mirror. "It's not what's on the outside that will make you sing," she said to her reflection, "but the inside that has always counted."

As Cherise brushed her teeth, she tried to believe the mantra; she tried to sink into the self-help platitudes deep inside her own subconscious, an amalgamation of synaptic pops and buzzes mixed with quotes from *O Magazine*. She spritzed perfume on her neck before washing most of the scent off with a moist cloth.

"No," she admonished her reflection, "you don't need French perfume to do this. We are recreating you from the ground up. At the end of the day," she promised her minty but apprehensive smile, which revealed a fine tangent of lines around her mouth, "you will be a unique, dare we say even *perfect,* woman."

She put on an old flowered dress and new cherry-red ballet flats. She slapped herself hard across each cheek the way she did every morning. Some mornings her bottom lip split. Sometimes this splitting made her late for her office job as she waited for the droplets of blood to thicken and fall off.

Cherise, in a rare act of defiance, decided not to go to work as she blotted a few drops of blood from her lips with a tissue. They probably wouldn't even notice her absence. What was one person in an ocean of assistant-assistants? She didn't eat lunch with any of the others, or take breaks at the same time. And her new cherry shoes deserved more than to be shoved under a cubicle all day.

Cherise wondered as she thought up an excuse to miss work if she would ever reach the point in a relationship that warranted an anniversary date to the symphony. This happened sometimes, these random thoughts as she dialed the number to call in sick.

After she typed in her work code and the automatic operator registered her absence, Cherise felt the urge to get out of herself, and her apartment. It wasn't that she didn't love her space, with its eat-in kitchen and its whitewashed brick accent wall and the way, if she strained on tiptoes out the bathroom window, she could almost see a monument so famous, its likeness took up residence in snow globes waiting to be shaken throughout the world.

Cherise wanted to see him. Her him. *Him*. And he wasn't the type of man to show up at her apartment uninvited. She must seek him out the way a flower seeks out spring. Yes, a flower. She would become the nectar, the stamen and the pistil, the unavoidable, desirous creature he had to have.

She avoided eye contact in the elevator, though she rode the mechanical tube alone, her reflection ready to stare back at her, throw her off track, disengage her from her goal as she dropped fifteen stories to meet the city floor. She wasn't going to use the word "sidewalk" anymore, part of her new uniqueness, preferring to view the asphalt and concrete that surrounded her as the bottom of an ocean, dark and permanent until something shifted—the familiar bus going by with a different advertisement shouting from its flank, a deli closing while a new café opened, a homeless man shuffling across her avenue to ask for change on the opposite street corner.

"Maybe I just need a new coat?" she asked the morning sunshine, a bluster of April breeze grabbing her flowered dress. The air stung her slapped cheeks and dug a needle into the fresh split on her lip, the one she knew would open to reveal more blood if she smiled. "Yes, you're right," she said, no stranger close enough to hear the mysterious other half of her conversation. "Candy is what I need. He likes candy, my man. Sweets for the sweet."

Cherise didn't mind the twenty-block walk to her favorite candy store. She passed diners serving omelets and a park with new grass and so many boutiques and bars and yogurt shops. Her shoes broke in. Another blessing in what she saw as a day ripe for surprise. A half hour later— for time passed differently as her new shoes stomped down the sidewalk, the newly malleable city floor, in time to the invocation "cherry red, cherry red"—Cherise considered changing her name to Cherry. The name fizzed with the effervescence of a Cherry Coke on a hot summer day combined with the sticky sweetness of a maraschino cherry balanced on a banana split. She believed that men liked to think about cherries and bananas; something she gathered when she tried that one time to view Internet porn objectively. She thought about calling herself Banana, then, but in Cherise's head it sounded like she was trying too hard, the fuzzy line between exceptional and desperate blurring more with each step.

Cherise felt blisters rise in sharp, insistent pain between her toes as she reached the candy store. Past the front door, the automatic cotton candy machine assaulted her with its blaring electronic calliope music. She watched a child feed money into the machine then devour the spun sugar in two bites.

"No, cotton candy won't do. I don't want to be known as the woman whose breath smells like a circus," Cherise said to the teenage girl who stood behind the counter, "or at least like a clown. I am looking for something unique. Something that will alert everyone, but most specifically the new and as yet unrevealed man of my dreams, that I am not only a woman to get to know, but a woman to hold near and dear for the rest of his life." She scanned the counter. "You know, two of hearts, till death do us part, that sort of thing."

"If you don't want cotton candy, I'd go with butter mints," the girl behind the counter answered.

"Excuse me?"

The girl pointed to a wall of bulk candy. "Brides-to-be buy butter mints in here all the time. They shove them in little plastic swans for party favors. Since you said you're getting married?"

"I didn't say that, and do you really think my dream lover will call my mouth a symphony when he sees me sucking like some puffer fish on a pillow mint?"

"What's a pillow mint?"

"You know, old candy you'd always find in Grandma's dish. When I was young, they were called pillow mints, I always assumed after the mouth of some famous actress. My grandmother kept a full glass dish on her piano."

The girl behind the counter said, "My grandma doesn't have a candy dish, but around Christmas she's really into playing that song about fig pudding."

"Yes, well." Cherise paused at the gelato counter and the display of handmade truffles. "I need something that I don't have to scoop from a bin and carry out of here in a plastic bag."

"What about Choward's mints?" The girl pointed to candy shaped like gum. "No one's bought a pack since I've worked here. That's been, like, at least seven months."

Cherise stared at the lemon mints in their bright canary foil and guava-flavored mints wrapped in sunset orange. Then she saw a purple glimmer hidden under piles of individually wrapped chocolate candies. When she smiled, she tasted blood.

"Oh," the girl said, "that's the violet flavor. No one's bought a pack of those, like, ever."

"Then I'll take all you have." Cherise opened her red patent leather purse, bought to match her ballet flats, and asked the girl to toss violet mints in by the handful.

She wondered what she was missing at work, if the coworkers who made fun of her for bringing lunch in a fabric-covered metal bin that matched each outfit would find someone new to harass. Cherise had made the bin from her mother's old flour canister, which she tucked fabric around each morning to coordinate her look of the day.

She wondered how someone who wore cherry-red ballet flats could ever be made fun of. Of course, she wished she lived in Paris, a different city that must look like the bottom of an even more exotic ocean floor, where other women named Cherise wore red ballet flats. To be unique in Paris, if she ever had the luck to travel the world, she vowed to wear green high heels and call herself "Banana."

Outside the store, Cherise ran her fingernail across the purple foil on a pack of mints. She stuck a violet candy in her mouth. Her lips erupted with the taste of perfume. Not a good taste or a taste she wanted to ever taste again. She spit the candy on the ground. As soon as it landed, Cherise bent to retrieve the lavender-colored square. Women who reinvented themselves did not litter. That was the old her.

The old her left trash around the city more from necessity than entitlement, rife as she was some mornings with the desire to hurt herself in ways no one would believe. Cherise never asked herself why she did the things she did, or whether others did them, too, a city silenced in its collective shame. She tried so hard not to rub against every sharp edge she felt on her way to work, to fight the compulsion, as she made her way through the city, to hike up her long skirts and expose her scarred flesh to more scarring. "Prudish skirts," her coworkers called them, as they bet right in front of her on whether she was old-fashioned enough to wear a girdle underneath, whether she shaved anything off or kept her body furred in the places that counted. Sometimes her coworkers even admitted she was pretty, and had a really nice mouth, a mouth men always seemed to notice, but she was just so weird, they all said, almost like she couldn't help it. No one had any idea how hard Cherise fought not to rub her bare legs against the elevator buttons, the escalator rails, the parking garage pylons, anything that would gouge her pale skin and leave tiny red trails running down her legs. She didn't want to be this way. She didn't want to litter if the tissues used to mop up her own blood, the tissues buried deep in whichever matching lunch bin she chose, piled up and peeked over the top of its custom-made straps.

The new Cherise hid the spit-out candy in one of her shoes by settling the fragrant disk between two blisters. "For today, for right now," she whispered, "I will be good to myself."

She unwound the purple foil and placed another candy on her tongue, this time easing into the taste of flowers as they overtook her mouth, not entirely unpleasant, very much like an alarming realization that she had accidentally swallowed perfume.

She gulped hard, spoke toward the bustle of the city in front of her, its souvenir shops and rival candy stores, the magazine kiosks that sold the best candy of all: "I am becoming the scent of violets. I am becoming a flower. I am becoming." She checked off turning her mouth into a symphony on her mental list. "My name is Banana," she said to an older woman who passed her on the street in a cloud of designer perfume.

The woman ignored her.

"I meant Cherry!" she yelled after the stranger. "You know," she pointed down, "like the color of my shoes!"

The woman and the cloud of perfume kept walking, didn't even turn back to remark on Banana-Cherry-Cherise's obvious odor of violets. Cherise tucked her roll of violet mints into her purse, walked back toward her apartment with that one mint rollicking between her sore toes. Four blocks into her journey, she stopped in front of a department store. She sat down on a bench and waited long enough to feel like she had missed her lunch break at work.

"New perfume. I almost forgot," she said to no one in particular as she left the bench a few hours later. So easy, really, to lose track of that kind of time. "Maybe wearing perfume won't make me unique, but wearing a perfume I would never normally choose might change something about me just enough to set off a chain reaction."

She entered the store, decorated in pearl garland and floral wallpaper, and sauntered to the closest perfume counter. The violet candy slipped from between her toes to become a smooth pebble rolling around inside her shoe. The perfume counter girl refused to look up from her arrangement of what Cherise called tattoo perfume, row after row of black and pink bottles decorated with tigers and hearts. The woman's nails shined bright as Chiclets, click-clacking against the counter as she rearranged the bottles in a strange game.

"What's the prize if you win?" Cherise asked. She called this new tactic toward her goal of uniqueness ingratiating herself with the people who worked at perfume counters. The man of her dreams would appreciate that.

"I work on commission." The woman grabbed a stack of perfume bottles created by a reality star and lined them up next to the others.

Cherise amped up her charm. "Of course I never learned Latin. Who did, right? But I wonder if the words 'commission' and 'commit' come from the same root, which basically means the same place."

"I know what root means."

"Of course you do. And if they do come from the same root, since both of us are so familiar with that sort of thing, are you essentially committing a crime by selling me things I don't really need, just to make your commission?" She tried to chuckle the way women on reality shows chuckle.

The girl behind the counter kept tapping her fingernails against the glass. She added the last perfume to the top of a perfume pyramid. "Is there something you'd like to try?" she asked when a manager appeared on the periphery.

Cherise pointed to a glass bottle filled with golden liquid. The color reminded her of a boat that could sail across the ocean for days, or maybe even the golden head of the ship's handsome captain. "I don't need to try because I already know I want that one right there. Is it rare?" she asked the perfume girl. "Because I'm looking for a scent that a starlet might mention in a fashion magazine, real off hand and secretive. Something that normal women wouldn't have access to unless they traveled to exotic celebrity locales, like Thailand or Williamsburg."

"Ma'am, it's Chanel."

"Why, you're right. I must've gotten so caught up in my own excitement, I forgot I actually used to do this for a living. There's nothing like a classic."

"I'm sure." The woman behind the counter wrapped the iconic white box that held the glass bottle in tissue paper. She placed the bottle in a bag with silk ribbon handles. "So is this reinvention to find Mr. Right?"

"I don't understand. How did you know I was looking for him?"

"Because you just told me about your boyfriend, like, two minutes ago," the woman said, "and how you've changed so much to accommodate him, but you used a prettier sounding word for accommodate."

"I did?"

"Yeah—how he works uptown as an investment banker and eats salmon for dinner three nights a week?" She scuttled her nails along the counter again. To Cherise they looked like ten miniature white-tipped tap shoes.

"Well, he does, and he does, and right now he's waiting for me." Cherise grabbed the bag. The violet mint lodged itself between two new toes. "He just doesn't know it yet."

"Your shoes match your bag; you're optimistic. That's half the battle," the woman said as Cherise left the store. "I hope you find your banker by happy hour."

Cherise knew what being made fun of sounded like. She'd always known, even walking through the world with her very pretty lips, that pretty lips were never enough. But the man who would call her mouth a symphony would never make fun of Cherise. He might tease her if she snorted a little when she laughed at old Marx Brothers movies, or tickle her in bed if she overslept when it was his turn to make pancakes. He would cut kernels off a cob to mix in scrambled eggs and it would sound weird on paper, but taste so good in real life. Like all great, private discoveries, no one else would understand the revelation of corn in scrambled eggs. Most of all, he wouldn't touch the cuts on her legs that never had time to heal before Cherise scratched new ones, sometimes so deep, as she leaned into the turnstiles before getting on the subway, that she cried out in pain.

The man who would call her mouth a symphony took his lunch break on a park bench only a few blocks from Cherise. She could feel him sitting there just out of reach as she removed the perfume, threw the ribbon-handled bag in the nearest trashcan, unwrapped the tissue paper in mock surprise of its contents, and doused herself. She tucked the bottle into her purse next to the violet mints.

"Of course you'll know every pulse point without having to ask," she said to the city street. "You always have and you always will, John."

John. Cherise knew the man who would call her mouth a symphony would be named John, just like that president who married a smart brunette but had sex with dumb blondes, and his son who rollerbladed all over town before marrying a smart brunette who died her hair dumb blonde. Cherise also suspected, as she continued her walk home, that men who thought about cherries and bananas also named their penises "John."

This didn't sound very unique.

Yes, Cherise knew, somewhere in her city John ate a turkey club on a park bench during his lunch break and wondered what sort of flower to tuck in the bouquet he would give her on their first date.

"My boyfriend—it really feels silly calling a man nearing forty a 'boyfriend,' though 'man friend' sounds like something a sailor would say, and John has never even sailed a paper boat across a pond," Cherise said to the owner of the Italian deli eight blocks from her apartment as she continued in the afternoon sun to wind her way home. "Like I was saying, John, my special friend, takes his lunch at noon. Since it's nearing three and he won't be home till six, do you have any recommendations for a little pick-me-up for our date tonight?" Then she pointed to her newly perfumed neck. "If this does the trick, of course we'll be staying in."

"I'll wrap you up a cream cake. It's just big enough to share."

Cherise knew men liked to talk about cherries and bananas. Thinking about cream, especially a cake filled with all that froth, must really turn them on. Even though she understood the way the male brain saw the world by analyzing each of their favorite words, one innocuous word at a time, Cherise hoped her uniqueness would materialize as more than just the ability to say words like "cherry" or "banana" with great conviction during the throes of passion.

She asked the deli owner, "Can you please be sure to put your delightful confection in a pink box and tie it with string? Since I was a little girl, I dreamed of carrying home a pink box tied with string."

"Miss, I think your lip is bleeding. You got a nasty cut. Who done that to you, anyway?"

"How can you not sense a feeling of potential clustering around a pink box tied in string?"

"You okay, miss? You need a napkin or something?"

"Oh yes, I'm just fine. Would you believe me if I told you I cut my lip this morning the same way I do every morning?"

"I don't believe it for a minute that someone as pretty as you would ever cut their own lip. Is it your boyfriend? If you tell me you bought an asshole like that the cake I make from my mother's recipe, I swear I'll..."

"No, it's me. It really is. I do it every day. Slap myself, cut myself, gouge the inside of my mouth with tweezers or the end of my toothbrush or even a drinking straw, if that's all I can find. And sometimes I punch myself so hard, a good body shot without flinching, I make myself sick."

"I don't believe that for a second."

Cherise thought of all the times she bled too much from cutting her thighs or poking her lips. Years before, when Cherise had friends, one of them kept asking who was beating her up all the time, how she could possibly stay with that kind of monster. Her friend, one of those women who even made brown mascara look sexy, told Cherise to get help.

"But there is no one to leave," Cherise tried to convince her. They drank coffee at a café near the office.

"So you're telling me you do this to yourself?" The woman's brown mascara lashes flitted like a hummingbird.

"Yes, and I also eat a chocolate brownie at least once a day." Cherise ordered another brownie from the barista.

"Eating too much chocolate means you aren't getting enough love in your life. Simple. What isn't so simple to figure out is your self-abuse."

Cherise wanted to tell her friend that she called her daily routine, the hard and quick slaps across her cheeks and lips while she gazed in her bathroom mirror, her "first movement." A way to begin each day the way a symphony begins. Quick, spirited, bright. Plus, she figured no one could hurt her if she hurt herself first.

"I'm being completely serious," Cherise said to the deli owner as she let thoughts of her old friend disappear. "And I want a pink box."

"We only have white boxes, and tape. No string." The deli owner placed a small white cake inside a matching box. "But this'll look real nice on a plate. Your man friend won't know what hit him when he comes home to not one, but *two* sweet treats."

"But I only asked you for one cake," Cherise said, before the man looked up from taping the white cake box shut and winked. "Oh," she giggled as the violet mint tumbled around in the shoes she nervously tapped on the floor, "you're talking about me."

"And are you sure you don't need to get help or anything?"

"Yes, thank you, but I'm very sure." She opened her hands to accept the cake box. Cherise wanted to tell the deli owner, almost handsome in a bloodstained, butcher-apron way, "Back in school they used to call me Banana," but he walked away to help another customer.

As the man sliced deli meat, Cherise walked into the bathroom. She pretended she wanted to adjust the cake box and her purse in private for the walk home. Once inside the small space, she untaped the cake box and thrust her hand deep into its bunny soft middle. Another compulsion, another uncontrollable ache. Cherise brought her hand to her lips, smearing them in white, greasy frosting before rubbing the leftover oil into the newest cuts on her thighs. Her lips, still sore from her first movement, stung as she licked the frosting off.

John probably didn't like cake anyway. He was one of those men who jogged during his lunch break and never used salad dressing. Before tossing the cake and its box into the bathroom trash, Cherise rubbed the edges of every finger over the waxy cardboard, cutting herself three times in three different spots. Drops of blood fell onto the snowy expanse of the sunken cake. Cherise tried to remember that one fairy tale about the girl with the fairest skin.

She would ask John to tell her the story before he tucked her in that night.

Cherise stared at the deli owner as she left his store, making the kind of deep, penetrating eye contact she only *imagined* being capable of pulling off. Only women with pretty, symmetrical faces, and not just very pretty lips, know how to make that kind of eye contact. She knew she could never go back to the deli once someone discovered the cake in the trash.

If Cherise wore a watch, she would have been the type of woman who only glances at her wrist if she knows someone is looking. Instead, she guessed the time by the way the violet mint continued to dissolve between her toes. It was already getting too late to shop for a new coat, bright green to match the high-heeled shoes she would someday wear when she moved to Paris and legally changed her name to Banana. John loved green because all men love green.

She was getting close to the apartment. The sun floated low in her city, the city that was really starting to feel like not just the bottom of the ocean, but the bottom of her own personal ocean, dark and unflappable as she bobbed along in her red ballet flats.

She reached her apartment in time to catch the lobby elevator without having to push the button. Maybe John was waiting inside for her, home from work two or three hours early. Maybe he brought a cream cake for them to share, and this time Cherise knew better than to stick her hand in the middle of dessert without at least asking first.

"John!" she called as she unlocked her apartment door and sashayed in. Her shoes almost felt comfortable as she zigzagged across the carpet. Cherise smiled wide enough to open the wound on her lip, tasting a morsel of her own iron as she shut the door behind her without locking it. On a side table, she set down her purse, heavy with her new perfume.

"John!" she yelled even louder. She walked through the modest living room toward the bedroom, where he must be waiting for her the way men who think too much about cherries and bananas always wait.

When she opened the bedroom door, no one was there. No one waited in Cherise's bedroom, bathroom, living room, adjacent kitchen with its seldom-used stove. She even opened the refrigerator and peered at the single-serving cans of vegetable juice and pickled beets. Months ago, Cherise was convinced those two ingredients would make the perfect, unique Bloody Mary the next morning if some-one ever stayed the night.

Cherise checked her front door to make sure she left it unlocked. John, of course caught up in the bank, was run-ning late. Or maybe he was a lawyer drafting torts; that other kind, not the chocolate kind.

Thinking of torts made Cherise hungry for the cake she had ditched at the deli. She wanted to slap her face to stop thinking about how she wasted that perfectly good cake.

"At least the deli owner'll believe the part about how I slap myself in the face now," she said to her empty apartment. "At least he'll believe me."

Cherise spritzed more cologne across her neck and wrists and even down the front of her thin flowered dress. She removed her ballet flats and tossed the tiny, nearly dissolved violet mint onto the floor before placing a new one on her tongue.

As the sun set in what looked out her window like a city view framed only for her, Cherise scanned the sidewalk several stories below. She waited for John to catch the scent of her new perfume, her violet mint, each and every one of her bloody, unknown secrets.

Selfie

Violet shuddered as another midnight breeze massaged its insistent fingers down her back. She had learned, after six nights in a row sitting in the cemetery, that midnight breeze has its own set of consequences.

Light wind before midnight kept Violet's senses on edge without plummeting her into nervous over-awareness. Her velvet bodices never constricted her breathing before midnight. Before midnight, her Dr. Marten eight-eye boots rubbed uncomfortable angles into her ankles, callused the tops and backs of both feet with their inability to wear in, though the blistery pain felt tolerable. Gothic fashion before function, as usual.

After midnight, her clothes felt so tight Violet's heart palpitated with the anticipation of some as-yet-unnamed creature crawling out from one of the nearest headstones, where she waited with the patience of statuary. Sometimes, before midnight, Violet pretended she was statuary.

A living, breathing, undead-looking woman with burgundy-black lipstick, loose face powder imported from China, black-dyed hair with blue highlights under the moon. Any number of big black boots. Single at thirty-two, never married, no kids, not even a man with a tattoo of her name on a regrettable body part, Violet made her living writing blogs about how to stay "Gothic" as middle age teetered on the edge of its own pair of patent leather platform shoes.

For having never left her small mountain town, Violet, through twice-daily posts, acquired followers as far away as Iceland. She believed those followers really did live in Iceland, rather than pretend they lived in Iceland, because they always posted pictures of lamb stew on Twitter and Facebook.

Her pen name, Raven Tresses, became synonymous in the underground scene with the virtual advice column to solve any myriad of Gothic-related concerns: Where do I buy black nail polish after October 31st? What did E.A. Poe really die from? What, Raven Tresses, is the correct way to pronounce Cthulhu, and can you please answer phonetically?

Violet had attended high school at Mountain Crest. She told her fans she majored in being a freak, with a minor in creative writing. Sometimes she posted scans of her teen-age poems, which never strayed far from retelling *Little Red Riding Hood* in favor of the wolf and *Hansel and Gretel* in favor of the witch. The impetus to create a blog began on Halloween a few years earlier, when Violet remembered her biology teacher, over a decade before, asking her in front of the whole class whether she was dressed up.

Teachers gave out "spirit points" for dressing up the week before Homecoming, Halloween included. The class with the most points won a pizza party. Dressing up was serious business.

"Today I am dressed like a witch," Violet remembered telling her teacher as she stared at the blackboard.

"How could anyone tell?" a kid behind her moppet of black hair asked. He laughed like a varsity football player figuring out which girl looked drunk enough to date rape.

The girl next to her, who only sat in that spot because the teacher assigned seats, asked Violet in the voice of Glinda from *The Wizard of Oz*, "Are you a good witch, or a bad witch?"

Violet stared at the tanned blonde girl who smelled like Sun-In and Jean Naté. "Why don't you come closer and see?"

In her inaugural blog, Violet detailed the girl, Sienna, with that irritating crayon name, whose looks, in reality, wouldn't even snag a weekend anchor spot on the local news. Such entitlement from such an ordinary face—the girl who felt so confident in her right to exist that she made fun of another girl in front of a crowded classroom.

Almost as soon as she posted that first entry, the collective consciousness sighed its black, misunderstood sigh back at Violet. Or maybe it was more like Violet's blog post raised the consciousness of others just like her, women nearing middle age with their Gothic hearts still intact, gloomy but not entirely broken.

In high school, Violet and her few friends had pretended to be unique, black lace-trimmed islands unto themselves, though each vampiric acolyte carried a spray-painted black lunchbox with Gashlycrumb Tinies cartoons découpaged on the sides. Most of her friends wore thick, smudged eyeliner and black lipstick; black petticoats, tights, boots, corsets; black velvet ribbons with Goodwill antique cameos. The more ordinary of their coven plastered their walls with Cure posters. One or two other girls, like Violet, listened to Bauhaus and Skinny Puppy, traded vials of their own blood—home-drawn from pricked fingers—with their equally misunderstood boyfriends. Those girls, including Violet, wrote the kinds of poems Sylvia Plath *wished* she could write.

"Plath was just another privileged New England bitch," one of her friends had said during lunch, their end of the cafeteria table perpetually bathed in black, highlighted by the biweekly piece of fruit thrown at them by the identical posse of football players.

"Privileged? But her father died of the sugar disease!" another answered.

"Can you please just call it diabetes?" Violet said. "Not every word out of your mouth has to be a dramatic monologue. And quit referring to avocados as 'butter pears,' or one of those asshole jocks will start throwing those, too. At least the apples and oranges don't splatter."

"Well, I don't think a father dying of diabetes equals a very privileged life."

"Are you kidding? She got to make up the line, 'Dying is an art' and sleep with Ted Hughes."

Violet's second blog post posed the question of whether or not Sylvia Plath was overrated. She did not expect a following. She actually expected no answers to her rhetorical question, tossed out into what felt like the pulsating blue vortex of her computer screen before being swallowed whole. Deep down she loved Sylvia Plath, or at least imagined being her best friend, in time to save her from forgetting to peroxide her hair and falling in love with a monster.

She did not call Ted Hughes a monster in her blog, afraid of being sued for libel.

That was how Violet began her quest, via what her few friends called the blogosphere, to document each of her dark, brooding days through an eternal round of selfies and posts, with a current emphasis on conjuring her own monster from its grave.

Comments lit up her page in a never-ending scroll of pro and con monster-hunting remarks. Typical bon mots included, "You can't conjure up a monster from a grave. They're all undead, you dumbass Gotho bitch." Or, "You suck more than Dracula." Or, "Zombies would starve around you."

Positive comments from followers with names like LizziesAxe and PlatinumBlondeDahlia encouraged Violet to take her darkness to the next level: "Quit listening to Robert Smith sing 'The Funeral Party' and have one yourself."

My followers are right, Violet thought as she posted tips on how to take the perfect selfie without the omnipresent Chinese face powder washing out carefully contemplated features. *No more lip service. I am going to meet my very own monster. And I am going to meet him tonight.*

She packed an antique carpetbag, won on eBay, with black taper candles, a small book of spells—though Violet doubted their authenticity, since she'd bought the book at Barnes and Noble—a small glass bottle of sparkling cider in case whatever creature made its presence known at the witching hour had alcohol intolerance, a makeup bag, a few Victorian-era cabinet cards, one small tintype also purchased on eBay, paper and crayons for grave rubbings, her portable record player, a recording of Toccata and Fugue in D minor, and, of course, her cell phone. Her followers would be waiting for her constant updates.

On her final post before setting out to spend her first night in the cemetery, she said, "Wish me luck. Next stop: undead."

The cemetery gate swung open without effort, a gravel path beneath the posts worn down by constant grieving. The town Violet came from was not famous for anything except not being famous for anything. In the late eighties, a rumor did circulate between her classmates that David Lynch almost filmed the *Twin Peaks* pilot there. One brief, close encounter with fame until her posts traveled as far away as Reykjavik.

Someday the people in charge might even ask her to join the Chamber of Commerce. They always asked blonde women who opened purse boutiques or independent bookstores. As the cemetery gate squeaked behind her, Violet wondered if the entire chamber was made up of purse-selling, bookselling blondes.

The cemetery closed at sundown. Violet and her followers knew she broke the rules, as all women do who put love before the law. Plus, as a lifelong Goth, she knew how to navigate out-of-bounds with a quiet swish of her velvet skirts. A few swigs of sparkling cider and a blog update complete with photo, and Violet sat down to wait near the headstone of a man who died in the Iraq war. This fact, though not stated on his sleek black granite, became more obvious when moonlight caressed an engraving of his death date and rank. Violet wondered if the man's spirit was the spirit the universe destined her to meet. Of course, the ghost of a dead solider was about as far away from a monster as Violet could get, but maybe *monster* was the wrong word, the wrong concept; much too sinister. Too, well, Gothic.

In flesh-and-blood life, the man, a boy really, was a decade younger than her when he died. Probably a high school athlete. No doubt a kid who would have thrown overly ripe "butter pears" at her cafeteria table, pilfered from his mother's stash softening in the pantry for taco night. But the afterlife, Violet assumed, must instill the kind of wisdom mere mortals cannot think their way past, plus answers to questions even a deep thinker like herself never thought to ask. Her solider, resurrected from his mortal slumber, would make the kind of blog post to end all blog posts.

As Violet waited for the man's ghost to appear, she practiced taking a few selfies in front of his headstone. She felt a presence standing near her in the dark.

"Hello?" she spoke into the night, right in the middle of what was going to be the best photo of the evening. "Is someone there?"

Maybe someone watched her behind that tree—how it curved into itself, how its pine needles shed along the cemetery floor in brown, prickly pallets. Do ghosts make their presence known? Can they be felt more than the belief that air chills when they come near, candles blow out, a pot of soup on the stove turns tepid? No—what Violet felt were real eyes on her, real eyes that her own gaze could not return. Or maybe the feeling, a feeling that touched her beneath the velvet, frosted her arms in gooseflesh, was nothing more than a late-night breeze?

She brushed off the sensation of being watched to practice interviewing herself for CNN. Maybe Anderson Cooper would fly in to meet the happy couple. She made a note to stock up on Starkist Tuna Creations. She guessed the silver-haired news anchor preferred his tuna in both the herb/garlic and hickory-smoked varieties. She read once how Anderson maintained his slim body by traveling with tuna. Violet also learned from the same article that serious news reporters call traveling for a story "going on location."

In her next blog post, Violet would call the cemetery her mobile "location."

Her cell phone clock glowed 2 a.m. in the mostly moonless night. Violet's body felt cold as the cemetery earth crept its wintry grasp up her velvet leggings to more velvet beneath. Or maybe what she felt was the slow process of apparition becoming body. From her portable record player, Toccata and Fugue in D minor echoed its menacing organ through the cemetery grounds. The nearest house sat too far away from the cemetery to be disturbed, and a butte ringed the other side. This was not the kind of cemetery that drew drunken teenagers to go down on each other behind the graves. Even on the foggiest nights, the cemetery sat quiet and still, plot after plot of bright plastic flowers resilient to the vagaries of weather. Of course, Violet wished to conjure something a little more ominous.

By 3 a.m., a time Violet's followers knew to be the true witching hour—not midnight, like most neophytes believed—her cell phone battery began to die without one appearance from anything remotely supernatural. No soldier ghost. No zombie. No wayward teen werewolf. She took a few photos of her record player, her half-empty bottle of cider, and then fell asleep leaning against the back of the soldier's grave.

The next day, home and showered and Shalimared, Violet scanned her blog comments. An overwhelming percentage of followers asked her not to give up her quest to find the most unnatural kind of love. And who would she be without her fans? So that night Violet packed more supplies, extra peanut butter and cracker snacks, and ventured back to the plots. Though she believed overexposure to be the death knell of celebrity—like Kanye buying Kim a thousand roses for Valentine's Day, which she posed in front of with her knees in the air—Violet toyed with the idea of announcing the start of her period. Not to overshare, but to begin a debate on whether menstrual blood might bring out the monsters. She passed her second night making grave rubbings of surrounding headstones until she ran out of paper and tampons. She ate every cracker snack before 2 a.m.

"Hello?" she called toward another tree, her mouth full of crackers. "Is someone there? If you're so intent on watching me, why don't you just show your face?"

Violet was sure this time, on this night, she had heard the shuffle of feet, or maybe even several pairs of feet, mere inches past where her sight failed in the dark. Wind couldn't possibly have its own sentient thoughts. Wind couldn't possibly choose which woman to watch eating crackers alone in a cemetery. Without anyone or anything coming forward, Violet sat by herself with her portable record player until sunrise.

On the sixth night, with no companion making his appearance under the blued moonlight, Violet, grimy from the cemetery dirt, gathered up her record player, her sixth empty cracker box, the tintype, the stub of her twelfth black taper candle. When she stood to dust off her velvet skirt, a voice said:

"Madame, you make very thorough rubbings. Most people who come here do not press hard enough."

She fought the urge to turn. She fought the urge to look. "Thank you," she said. "I played with Fashion Plates as a child."

The male voice, a voice Violet guessed would possess the recognizable quality of an Eastern European accent as she waited for every W to become a V, said, "Vhat are these Fashion Plates you speak of?"

"You know," she slowly turned to see a tall, pale man in velvet standing behind a gravestone, "you arrange a piece of paper onto the template of a pretend fashion model, then color in their clothes by pressing a crayon just so." Her black lace cuffs ruffled in the breeze as she mimed the movement of an invisible crayon.

"Very in-ter-est-ing."

He sounded exactly like she knew he would.

Violet took out her phone to snap a picture in the man's direction without being obvious. The man seemed to float closer, seemed to glide toward Violet and her record player and her carpetbag and her empty cracker box without moving his feet. Of course he wore a dark velvet cape and a silver medallion.

"Pardon me," she asked the man, "but do you happen to be a creature of the night? Are you the one I've almost seen out of the corner of my left eye, watching me each night but never getting close?"

"My, are not you a bold one. And no, I am afraid I just flew in tonight. I mean, I just arrived this ev-en-ing. But rest assured, dear one, I vould have made your acquaintance days ago if I knew you vere here vaiting."

The man came close. He was nothing like a character in one of those teen books her followers boycotted, with vampires cold to the touch who shined like diamonds in the sun. "And I don't suppose you pal around with werewolves, either," she asked the intoxicating creature.

"Oh, goodness, no. How gauche."

Violet introduced herself to the man by snapping a selfie with his pale outline towering above her powdered face. She strained to frame his ethereal movements in the shot and posted the picture without seeing if it turned out. One more selfie, a little closer, which Violet did not even glance at to evaluate composition or form before hitting the share button. The man took the phone from her hands.

"I didn't mean to be rude." She looked into his black eyes. "I'm just kind of on the clock right now."

"How could any facet of you seem anything but perfectly lovely?" he asked. "And tell me more about this clock."

Violet and the man, who called himself Tobias, never Toby for short, not even by his closest friends, both "dead and undead," strolled out of the cemetery hours before daybreak and its potentially lethal sun. He carried her record player by its plastic handle and her carpetbag in his other long, thin hand.

"Vhere are ve off to now, my dear one?"

"Well, I figure we should get you inside before the sun comes out. Am I correct?"

He switched the record player and carpetbag to opposite hands. "Yes, how very, very right you are."

At Violet's house, she drew the brocade curtains in each room by untying multiple gold-braided cords. She poured two glasses of cranberry juice, fully aware of the poor substitution for blood. After handing the man a glass, she checked the mousetraps set in the laundry room. Tobias took care of a furry offering in one of the traps while Violet agreed to wait in the bathroom, relieved she was over her period.

Without mentioning the small but necessary laundry room slaughter, Violet invited Tobias into her bed. There was no music. The new couple did not need candlelight flickering along the walls. Making love to a vampire felt like making love to a piece of art. Tobias aroused each sense without overwhelming her, knew exactly what Violet wanted to hear and exactly how to say it. What struck her more than his deft movements, his perpetually dilated pupils, his expected tendency to bite her in a way that almost felt threatening, was how Tobias snuggled against her body after they both felt satisfied.

"I love you," he whispered into her ear. "And after ve slumber the rest of the day and deep into the night, I will awaken and cook for you the red velvet pancakes."

Sleeping next to a vampire, wrapped in the shroud of his arms, incited the strangest dreams Violet could ever remember. Good dreams of wildflower fields and all-you-can-eat spaghetti buffets and wearing a bikini without shame and listening to the *Cabaret* movie soundtrack on continuous repeat.

In the morning, when Violet awoke to a doughy, chocolaty smell, she thought she was still dreaming. When she stared at the sight of blood-red pancakes stacked on the good china near the end of the bed, Tobias showed her the empty bottle of red food coloring. They both chuckled. She followed him into the kitchen, where he stirred together the ingredients for cream cheese glaze with a long fingernail before excusing himself to the laundry room again.

Violet took a selfie of pancake eating. She captioned the photo, "Vampire + sleepover = pancake party!" Comments ignited her blog moments later. Female fans exhibited a tendency to want to believe her story. Male fans demanded proof.

"Show us a picture!"

"Vlad the Impaler or hoax? #bogusfangs"

"Either show us a picture or I'm unsubscribing."

On the grocery list held with a Misfits Crimson Ghost magnet to her refrigerator, an elegant script had penned in calligraphy: steak tartar, liver, kidneys, garlic-free spaghetti sauce, mousetraps.

"Tobias, could you come in here please?"

Before she finished her sentence, the creature stood at attention by her side. "My dear Violet, do you require more pancakes, more carnal pleasures, more carrying of your record player and your carpetbag?"

"No, no, nothing like that. Not that all those things aren't wonderful, and not like I'm not grateful for you following me home..."

"How could I not follow you home? You are a goddess who valks the earth, a supreme voman, a queen among queens, to whom I pledge my loyalty for eternity and far, far beyond."

Violet took her phone from the black velvet coin purse she tied around her wrist each morning as part of her Gothic ablutions. "That's all fine and good, but can I take your photo for my blog now? I swear it'll take less than a second—then on to more pancakes and more of whatever goes on in the laundry room."

When she held the phone in front of her, smile perfected from the thousand other pictures Violet had taken of herself, she did not see Tobias's image on the screen.

"There must be some mistake." She pointed to her phone. "What an annoying technical glitch."

"Technical? Glitch?" Tobias polished the monogrammed brass buttons that ran down both sides of his shirtsleeves.

"You aren't showing up in the photos. Look," Violet pointed to her computer. "Each time I post a photo, what should be a shot of us as a happy couple becomes a selfie."

"Selfie?"

"You know, a photo of just myself."

"I do not see how that could ever be a bad thing." Tobias stared at Violet's neck. "Is it time to check the mousetraps yet?"

"Not quite yet."

As she deconstructed her blog, each selfie bold and emphatic where Tobias should be, Violet examined her reflection, a black-laced negative. But though her new special friend crept close enough for his fangs to graze her left ear, Tobias did not reflect in the computer screen.

"I vas afraid you vould notice."

"Notice?" Violet scooted an inch away from the creature's overly warm breath, his sharp nibbling on her earlobe, the tiny drops of blood he apologized for coaxing to the surface of her pinna one glorious corpuscle at a time.

"I cannot be photographed. And believe my most solemn truth, you are not the first in my five hundred and eighteen years to try. I almost thought somebody like you vould already know."

"No, I didn't know. But now my fans most certainly do."

One word stuck out on a quick scan of Violet's blog comments: poser.

Poser, death to Gothic fandom. Once you are labeled a poser, you better kiss your street cred goodbye. Johnny Cash giving the finger before performing in San Quentin Prison in 1969: cool. Eddie Vedder paying tribute to Kurt Cobain on *Saturday Night Live* by pointing to a magic marker "K" scrawled on the T-shirt he wore under his flannel: poser. R.E.M's "It's the End of the World as We Know It (And I Feel Fine)": cool. Billy Joel's "We Didn't Start the Fire": poser. The Clash: unabashedly cool. Green Day: extreme posers.

Violet had worked too hard for too many years and avoided being hit by too many pieces of fruit to let one five-letter word destroy her. It took more effort than anyone but another Goth could imagine. How many people knew how hard it was to iron velvet leggings? Line a top lip into sharp black triangles? Pretend to have not only read, understood, and enjoyed H.P Lovecraft, but refer to him in casual conversation as "Howard," just like Patti Smith did in that one interview?

Violet refused to let a pancake and lovemaking creature of the night screw things up for her, no matter how charming and handsome and kind.

"Come here. Let's try something." Powder clung to Tobias's translucent cheeks as Violet attempted to make him camera ready. "And maybe you are wearing too much black?"

"Too much black?"

"Shh, just be patient."

She dressed Tobias in a white button-up shirt and wrapped a white scarf around his neck. In one of his slender hands she placed a plate of half-eaten red velvet pancakes;

in the other, the withered corpse of a mouse, the appetizer Tobias had recently sucked dry.

Click. Click. Zoom in. Steady. Click. Click. Click... nothing.

"Nice try, poser," the blog comments said, "and we're reporting you to the ASPCA for what you did to that poor mouse!"

"I can't believe this," Violet said toward the computer screen. "I finally find someone who makes me happy and no one else can see him, at least not on any form of social media."

That night she asked Tobias to sleep on the couch, her withdrawal of him harder because she craved what his body could do to her body. She yearned for his calculatingly pleasurable touch, how his accent sounded almost fake, like when Liam Neeson plays a character in a movie who has to save someone from something. Even though she kicked him out of her bed, Violet awoke in the morning to Tobias waiting for bubbles to appear around the edge of each red velvet pancake before he flipped. He wore a pair of boxers that showed off his lean physique and her TEAM NOSFERATU T-shirt.

"I hope you do not mind," he said over the aroma of chocolate cakes. "I saw another one that said TEAM EDWARD, but I do not know who that is."

"Never mind that," Violet said, hoping her TEAM JACOB T-shirt and her *Twilight* phase would go unnoticed.

Tobias moved around the small kitchen with the dexterity of Rudolph Nureyev. "How many breakfast cakes does my lovely desire this fine morning?"

"None, but thanks." Violet turned on the computer. She clicked on her blog page and waited for the comments to refresh.

"Are you not hungry, my darling?"

"It's not that." Her velvet morning clothes felt cumbersome, the petticoat beneath scratchy and unyielding.

"It is because ve did not vork up your appetite like ve did the night before."

"Yes, that is quite true." She stared at Tobias. "And maybe this is all impossible for me to ever explain."

Violet gathered Tobias's folded clothes and cufflinks into a paper bag.

He stopped flipping pancakes. Quickly the smell of burnt batter filled the room. "Is it the mice?" he asked in the voice of a child about to be punished. "Because I cannot really help things like that."

"No, it's not the mice, or my cat."

Tobias stared at the kitchen floor. "Oh. You vere not supposed to notice that."

"It's okay. Really, I do understand. It's just that my fans never will."

"Can I keep your T-shirt? I have not had a new garment in at least two hundred years."

The couple waited until nightfall. They spent the day watching Francis Ford Coppola's *Dracula* ("Vhat? This is very, how you say, fake.") and *Love at First Bite* ("Oh, I love the disco dancing scene most of all!"). At dusk, Tobias and Violet walked to the cemetery hand in hand. This time his other hand did not carry her carpetbag. At the cemetery's middle, near the tree where she swore, nights before, a presence had watched her in the blackness, the couple said goodbye to each other. Before disappearing behind the tree, Tobias waved the way a lover waves when he assumes, incorrectly, that someday he will be invited back.

Violet snapped selfies of her tears. She posted the wet-tracked close-ups. Her nose ran onto her lips but she continued to pose. She hoped the pictures captured the grief and dedication of pleasing her fans above all else. She hoped the pictures conveyed the tragic story of a love that could never work in the digital age. She hoped the grief of star-crossed lovers would cause both Twitter and Facebook to crash.

The thing that waited for Violet, had waited for Violet since she left the cemetery days before, just out of reach behind its favorite tree, hoped the woman who kept staring into her strange little machine would forget to look up and see it coming.

Happy Anniversary

Thomas pulled his car onto the shoulder of the familiar desert highway. From the side of the road, his wife retracted her upturned thumb as he patted his chest to make sure this year's gold anniversary charm waited patiently in his shirt pocket. Thomas would not give Emma her gift until the conclusion of The Game. He rolled down the passenger window.

"Am I doing it right?" Emma asked as she bent and stuck her head through the open window.

"No questions, remember?"

Thomas had conceived of The Game as he and his wife planned their tenth overnight trip to the central Oregon desert. On each anniversary, they took a long weekend from his job as community college English professor and her job as a library assistant to load their car with birdwatching binoculars, a picnic lunch, and their worn book about Summer Lake.

Each year as they loaded the car, Thomas dissected the contents of the lunch Emma arranged in a picnic basket, another one of the sentimental icons she insisted they use for what she called their "Happy Anniversary Trip." He pondered the same brand of barbecue beans, the same turkey pita sandwich, the same beer—four bottles to split between them—followed by one square of chocolate cake.

It was Thomas's ongoing contempt for the chocolate cake that first inspired The Game. Emma bought the pre-packaged slice from the same grocery store and convinced the head baker to tape one blue birthday candle to its plastic container. Each anniversary, Emma waited until her husband's final swallow of beer to present Thomas with the cake. She swatted mosquitoes away from her sagging curls on the porch of the cabin they rented and launched into the Happy Birthday Song, though she substituted the words "Happy Anniversary."

Year nine had sent Thomas over the edge.

"I've had enough of everything always being the same," he had said, in the middle of Emma's operatic Happy Anniversary solo while the birthday candle shed its blue wax.

"Thomas, calm down. The people in the next cabin over will think something's wrong."

He extinguished the flaming wick between two fingers. "Not only is something wrong. Everything is wrong!"

Her gold bracelet with its nine gold charms jangled as Emma stood, following him into the cabin. "But I thought everything was fine?" she questioned the small, buggy expanse. "Except we left our dinner plates outside. I just know by morning some kind of animal will drag those watermelon rinds into someone's camp."

Outside, the desert glowed with an unobstructed sunset. A famous natural hot spring invited visitors from around the state to soak up minerals as the sun went down and the main building, a short walk from the cabin, became clothing optional. In almost a decade, the couple had never placed one collective toe in the water. In equal parts, Emma feared both nudity and other people's germs. Thomas never accepted the concept of water, from baptism on, as being able to cure anything.

"Let me get around you, Tommy. I need to clean up."

"See what I mean?" Thomas grabbed for his wife but hooked his finger on her Eiffel Tower charm, an anniversary gift from years ago, when standing in line all day to see the Mona Lisa still seemed like a good idea.

"No, Tommy, I don't."

Thomas strained in the impending darkness to make out the face and body he knew better than his own. He whispered toward what he thought was his wife's ear, "But don't you remember how small she looked in person? And how very far away?"

Emma found her husband's shape in the dark. She kissed him with her patented dry, slow kiss that always lasted one beat too long. "My poor baby. All those years ago and you're still—"

"I'm still nothing! And it was only four years ago, by the way, and those people were all crowded around Mona Lisa, taking her picture, smelling of sweat and fast food."

"It wasn't exactly fast food. It was Starbucks, remember?"

"Of course I remember."

"And my darling still can't accept that one should never try turning myths into reality."

Thomas longed to ask his wife, as she scurried from his grip toward the threat of watermelon rinds marring their front porch, "Then what's the point of marriage?"

A year later, the car idled on the side of a sage-brush-lined, two-lane highway. Emma held up her thumb again in a half-hearted attempt to hitch.

She said, "I swear I can pretend to be someone else for the whole night. Why don't you turn the car around and come back to get me again?" Emma pointed to the road, the chance for Thomas to spend the night with a glorious new stranger unfolding the warm and certain way a desert highway unfolds. Her charm bracelet chimed a symphony in the desert's swift breeze.

"First, give me your bracelet."

Emma instinctively covered her left wrist. She never took the bracelet off, ever. Another sentiment in what Thomas was beginning to see as the syrupy, self-pitying way his wife gave every object a crucial, symbolic imperative.

"I am taking off your bracelet." Thomas reached over and unhooked the heavy gilt band Emma surrendered by dangling her flushed wrist through the open passenger window. She could barely reach her husband's insistent fingers. "I won't be able to pretend you are a stranger to me and I am a stranger to you if I keep seeing things that remind me."

"But doesn't everything about me remind you?"

"I also can't play The Game if I'm irritated."

"Tommy, baby, why don't I grab you a sandwich? You have that glazed look you get when your blood sugar drops."

"Goddamn it, Emma, how can I make you understand that for the next twenty-four hours, you do not know that I am prone to low blood sugar. You have not made sandwiches.

In fact, you don't even know we are going to spend a night in a cabin. The moment I turn this car around, you will become a new woman and I will become a new man. We will be new to each other, like we were a decade ago."

"Except you also want me to pretend to be a hooker?"

"Now you just sound crass. You know I never specifically said that."

"I guess you didn't."

Thomas drove away from his wife. Emma stared at the red bubbles of pain blistering the backs of her heels. Thomas had surprised her with new shoes, black stilettos because he was not well versed enough in role-playing to choose a truly exotic kitten heel dolloped in marabou. The shoes cut into Emma's feet as she wobbled along the side of the highway.

Moments later, her husband, now no longer her husband, appeared. Again, he stopped his car on the shoulder. "You need a ride?" he asked Emma.

She got in the car. "Name's Rose. You?"

"Edward, but everyone calls me Teddy."

So much like Thomas. Already the gears of The Game needed oiling as he drove toward the anniversary cabin. Emma, now Rose, stared ahead. The alkaline lake came into view. Thomas glanced at Emma, now Rose, as he neared their turnoff. Rose loosened the belt on her summer dress.

"Nice to meet you, Edward but everyone calls me Teddy. Like the Kennedy who let that poor girl drown in a place that looks a lot like this one?"

"If you're referring to Chappaquiddick, nobody ever proved a thing."

Thomas waited for his wife to agree with him before he remembered the woman who sat next to him was no longer his wife. The ever-agreeable Emma, the dutiful woman who went along with The Game without protest, had already disappeared.

"I don't know if you heard me the first time," Thomas said as they reached the turnoff for the hot springs resort, "with the wind blowing so hard, but I was saying how that lake you were referring to isn't dangerous any more than a Kennedy is dangerous."

"I bet that poor drowned girl disagrees."

Rose grabbed the picnic basket from behind her seat. She opened the basket and dragged her nails through its fluff of paper towels and turkey sandwich and piece of chocolate cake before dumping the contents out her open window onto the highway shoulder. She replaced the basket behind her seat.

A moment later, too quick for Thomas to respond to anything, she yelled, "Stop!"

"Stop? Stop what?"

"Come on, let's get out here and explore. I'm feeling the urge."

"But you've never asked to stop here before," Thomas said.

"I've actually never been here. You must have me confused with someone else."

Thomas stopped the car at the entrance to a pioneer cemetery. "Yes, of course. My mistake."

From the gravel side road, he could see the anniversary cabin waiting for them in the near distance. The car pinged in the heat. Thomas wondered if some necessary part of the perplexing engine was overheating. Rose reapplied orange-red lipstick while examining herself in a compact Thomas could not remember ever seeing before.

Thomas followed this stiletto-heeled vision toward the nearest crumbling gravestone. Rose stopped to remove her heels. She pointed to the lake, so still and clear and blue it looked painted onto the surrounding desert expanse. "Aren't we going to do what you brought me out here for now?" she asked.

Birds flew over the stagnant water as if they were painted, too. Beyond the graveyard Thomas could smell the lake, a fishy undercurrent as if another creature just like Rose, too fantastical to tie down, hid beneath the surface.

"Come on, already." Rose beckoned Thomas, never really Teddy, to follow her to the only grove of trees within miles. "If we keep going past the cemetery, we'll walk straight into the water."

"But it feels like the further we walk, the further away it is." Thomas pointed to their cabin, number three on a plot of five cabins, each named for a native plant. Sun danced off the metal roof of The Manzanita.

Rose stopped walking but did not follow his hand. Thomas wondered what this new entity was thinking. He always knew, or pretended to know, Emma's thoughts, about the last book she read or the chicken recipe she was known for or what she would say when they passed through any small town.

"Oh, Tommy, doesn't this look like something out of *The Twilight Zone?* You know the one I'm talking about."

And Thomas knew, because Emma only ever mentioned one episode of the classic sci-fi TV show. She equated an abandoned gas pump or a park gazebo ringed in sleepy late-spring daffodils or a soda fountain with hand-scooped milkshakes, or even a certain man crossing the street in just a certain way, to something out of her past, or more like an occurrence she wished she could claim from her past, a chimera revisited over and over until it became dogmatic, more ritual than thought.

"Looks like someone's come down with a nasty bit of nostalgia again," he always said as he kept driving, anxious to arrive at the next destination before feeling equally anxious to keep moving forward.

"I'm not a very nostalgic person," Rose answered.

Thomas did not realize he had spoken out loud.

Rose said, "In fact, I usually pretend the past belongs to someone else and that I only exist in the present. Now, unbutton your pants and take out your cock."

Rose said the word Thomas had begged Emma to utter since their third date. It figured, he thought, that the compass of his romantic relationships would calibrate True North with a woman who needed two lemon drop martinis to even say the word "penis." To her it was always "your thing," as in, "Let me see your thing," or once every year or so, "Show me your erection," but only after too many (one and a half) White Russians at a faculty Christmas party. She attributed her inability to dirty talk to the fact that, having educated herself to guard a literal library, words were much too precious to pervert.

Sometimes Thomas yelled at Emma when she called his manhood "The Thing," "I'm sick of there never being a cock or a cunt between us!"

"Well, I don't like hearing either C word. They both really give me the creeps," Emma always said. With lotioned hands, she would knead Thomas's "thing" then, until it was not a thing at all. Without missing a stroke, unfazed by how the more she manipulated Thomas, the less desire filled his body, Emma said some domestic variation of, "Did I tell you Jackie and Dale converted a claw-foot bathtub into a loveseat? I know you've always thought Dale was kind of gayish, but he sure knows his way around a power tool."

Thomas would strain to stay aroused by the sound of Emma's little ruby mouth saying the word "tool." He gave up, as always, and asked her to stop. She turned from him in bed to read Jane Austen.

Rose didn't read books. Of course she knew how to read. It just wasn't her "thing."

"It's like that line about bad girls being too busy to keep a diary," she said when Thomas asked. "Now show me your cock."

"Can't we at least kiss a little first? Get to know each other a bit?"

Rose manipulated her summer dress to fit tighter around her breasts. She watched a dragonfly land near a cemetery fencepost.

Thomas walked toward Rose and her dress. "I mean, with that gorgeous mouth of yours, I'm sure it would be fun."

"I only kiss people I feel close to. Kissing is very intimate."

Thomas felt dizzy. This was The Game cranked in full gear. He clung to the strange, anonymous distance. "I understand. A lot of people would argue this, but I have always found kissing the most intimate act of all. Why don't we revisit this again later? Maybe tonight, as the sun sets and we're toasting each other with a glass of our favorite wine. Who knows where the night will lead us, right?"

"No. I don't mean it will take more time with you." Rose's great, dark eyes stared at Thomas. "What I meant to say is that I can tell I will never feel close to you. Now, like I said before, show me your cock."

Thomas undid his belt and unzipped his khaki pants. Before he could ask Rose if she really wanted to have sex with him for the first time under an oasis of poplars instead of their very nice, very expensive cabin, she got down on her knees. Everything was over before it began.

When she was finished Rose didn't even rinse out her mouth in the salty tributaries. She stood and smoothed sections of her frizzing hair behind each ear. "That seemed pretty painless. Now what do you want to do?"

The ten-year anniversary charm in Thomas's front pocket carried on an illicit affair with his Swiss Army knife. The tiny pony bucked against the knife as if it wanted to brandish its gold coating onto the European efficiency of its pocket mate. Thomas placed no symbolism on the horse. When he purchased the charm from the jewelry store, where he bought each year's offering, he instantly forgot if he intended to tell his wife that the token represented a thoroughbred racehorse, some correlation between an animal cultivated to cross a finish line and a marriage a decade into the blueprint of a content, domestic life.

Thomas wanted to stop The Game. Hearing Rose describe pleasuring him as "pretty painless" had somehow changed things.

"I think that's enough, Emma. We've had our hour of fun. Why don't we have a picnic under that tree, then go check into our cabin for a nap before dinner?"

The woman, Thomas's woman, whose eyes usually looked so sad with their perpetual, deep-set shadow, now stared him down with fortitude. "Why did you just call me Emma?" she asked while Thomas fumbled to tuck himself away.

"Very funny. And since you're still barefoot, why don't I grab the sandwiches?"

"I threw your sandwiches out the window." Rose retied the belt that cut an umber slash through her torso.

"But what about my hypoglycemia? You know I get strange when I don't eat enough."

Rose stared in the direction of the anniversary cabin.

Thomas asked, "Why did you do that, anyway?"

"Just because, I guess."

"Okay that's enough. I'm calling off The Game right now." Thomas walked toward the car. Lightheaded from the unrelenting high desert sun and the way Rose had taken him into her mouth, he hated how she watched him stagger. This is how it must feel to prance around in those ridiculous high heels.

A soft but adamant voice asked, "But, Teddy, don't you want to take me to a real bed? What I just did was only an *amuse-bouche*."

Emma! For a moment Thomas recognized the involuntary Germanic sensibility that flattened and desexualized her attempt to speak any Romance language.

"Well," he said, "I mean, we did, I mean to say *I* did, already pay for the night."

"Oh yes, then let's."

Thomas got into the car. Rose climbed in next to him and tucked her right leg under her body. Emma would never sit with her right leg tucked under her body. The couple drove to the cabin resort. Summer Lake bubbled its slow, sulfured lurch close enough to shy away from.

"Do you like poems?" Rose asked.

Thomas parked the car in front of their cabin. "Sometimes I do. It really depends on which poem."

Rose unwrapped too many pieces of bubblegum. She shoved the powdery pink rectangles in her mouth without offering any to Thomas. "I like best the one about the man who carries his lover's heart around in his heart, for safekeeping." In college, Emma minored in American literature with an emphasis on modern poetry. With a mouthful of gum, Rose said between chews, "But I've only read, like, three or four poems in my entire life."

"You're talking about e.e. cummings."

"Nah, never heard of him before."

Nausea rose from Thomas's stomach. If Rose, nee Emma, could already, in the course of two hours, lie without blinking the messy caterpillars of her smudged mascara, didn't that mean she was a pro at deception? What about Emma's "platonic" male friends, as she called them, a clinical word Thomas hated, for to insist the man who helped her catalog new library books into the computer system was only a Tuesday lunch date and nothing more, or how Ray from the pool "only sees me as a friend," meant thoughts of sex were already being considered, and denied. Guilt by breaststroke. Guilt by tuna salad sandwich.

Rose hopped from the car. She skipped, still barefoot, toward the cabin. "Oh, Teddy, hurry, let's go to the hot spring. Doesn't that sound fun?"

"But we never hot spring." He trailed after the sweat-dampened curls and shock of bright lipstick as Rose slammed the cabin door behind her, leaving him on the front walk.

Inside the cabin she yanked open the muslin curtain and stripped off her summer dress. Thomas knew other vacationers could see his wife changing in the small room, the room the couple had made hasty, muffled love in each year. Rose's body glowed from a lamp on the cabin side table, yellow shadows gilding her curves. Through the window the sunset flattered a form still firm in the best places but soft around the waist, almost as if something had fallen and settled there. Normally self-conscious of what Emma called her "pooch," Rose bloomed before the open window. She alternated stretching each arm over her head before bending to compress her gut into a ripe thickness that, for the very first time, Thomas wanted to bite into instead of pass over with the polite aversion good husbands train themselves to master.

Without acknowledging Thomas's eyes, Rose lounged on the bed. Her breasts, with their accustomed middle-aged sway, their treasure of intricate nerves Thomas had years ago grown bored of igniting, now sprawled on the bedspread like an invitation, the woman he spied through the paned cabin window no less enticing than what Thomas, and every other man like him, called *those women*. He imagined a curtain pulled up just for him as he leered at the woman behind the glass, willing to pay money to glimpse her upper thigh and the hidden, furry promise of so much more.

"Is that really you?" he mouthed toward the window-pane.

Darkness inked the world around Rose's golden peepshow. She turned from him to roll off the bed and began to walk toward him. He ran to answer her nudity at the cabin's front door.

"You can't come out here like this, Emma. What if someone sees you?"

"I was only going to grab my overnight bag. And quit calling me Emma. If you don't loosen up, I'm gonna start calling you Grandpa. Why don't we test out those waters now?"

The resort owners channeled the hot springs through a series of rudimentary aqueducts into a swimming pool inside an aluminum barn lit by a strand of Christmas lights.

"Rose," he said, without having to translate the foreign language of familiarity into another woman's name, "why don't we wait until the springs are clothing optional? We could grab a quick drink in town first."

"That sounds fun," Rose said.

Thomas scuttled her like a lost mermaid back into the cabin. Rose shimmied into her summer dress. Thomas forced himself not to touch the small sweat mark darkening her lower back as she turned from him to find her shoes.

"I'm afraid my feet hurt too much to wear any."

Thomas ran cool water from the cabin tap onto the top of his head. "And you didn't bring any others?" he asked her between streams of relief.

"I only wear stilettos."

A vision of their mudroom at home, laden with Emma's collection that felt good but looked like multiple, slightly varied garden shoes, made Thomas want to cry. He regretted every time he had ignored Emma when she came home from the library for the simple fact that he hated how his own wife did not care how she looked.

Rose reapplied her garish pout. Thomas missed his wife's sensible shoes and her turkey pita sandwiches stuffed with sprouts and her carefully cultivated syllables, which never stuttered into each another.

*   *   *

They drove five miles to Paisley, a post office and one-tavern town famous for a late summer mosquito festival. Rose skipped across the tavern parking lot in her bare feet.

"I bet all that moribund water is like manna to those pests," Thomas said as the couple entered the bar. He enjoyed flexing his vocabulary inside a place that served chicken tenders.

They seated themselves near the screened front porch. A brief exhale of recognition passed between them—but why would Emma come back if she really could exist as Rose the rest of her life, the kind of woman who spent extra money, which she never had much of, on strawberries during those central Oregon winters when a tiny, withered pint cost more than a meal in an expensive restaurant? Rose was the kind of woman who bought strawberries in winter and wore too much eyeliner and heady French perfume, even in a town like Paisley.

Thomas wondered what it felt like to be Emma, a woman he sometimes forgot to kiss goodnight, a woman known for how she cooked chicken.

"Do you just want to get a beer?" he asked.

Under the bar table, Rose dragged her dirty heel across Thomas's calf. "Let's order a basket of fries or something. I'm famished. Did you see that sign over there? The men are all in back playing poker, like we're in some sort of alternate, segregated universe. Why don't you join in?"

"But I came here to be with you." Thomas used his shoe to knock Rose's foot off his shin.

"We both know that isn't true. You'd have a lot more fun tonight if you just accept this for what it is."

Rose ordered a deep-fried platter. Neither of them spoke. Rose asked the waitress for extra Ranch dressing and complimented her engagement ring when the woman returned with a smaller plastic basket filled with dipping sauce.

"Look at that." Thomas pointed to the basket. "Chipotle has even arrived in this one-horse town."

The sauces dripped off Rose's chin as she munched on deep-fried mozzarella sticks that separated from their breading to stain her summer dress. She looked like a woman newly introduced to the intoxicating pleasures of food.

"This is, like, so fucking good I can hardly contain myself." Rose sucked on both of her thumbs at once.

Thomas grabbed a handful of napkins from the table dispenser. "Jesus, slow down."

"How come?"

"Because you're making a scene. And quit Goddamn swearing in here."

Thomas wiped Rose's chin.

Rose's doll eyes focused over the top of his head on another flyer advertising poker night. "You look a little nauseous," she said between bites. "But I still think you should saunter your overly educated brain back there and try to wow the yokals with a royal flush."

From the jukebox, a woman with an emphatic twang sang about some girl who left her suds in a bucket and her clothes on a line. "Come on," Thomas said around a mouthful of fried zucchini. "Do you know any woman who still dries her clothes on a line?"

Rose focused on him. Thomas felt like he received first contact from another planet when she asked, "What do you mean?"

"Oh, nothing. Just a line in that horrible song we just heard."

The waitress brought them each another beer. Rose dragged a fry through a light pink sauce. "Wasn't it another one of those *I am woman hear me roar because you done me so wrong I still want to make love to you* songs?"

"Something like that."

"I bet every time a station plays a country song, Betty Friedan turns over in her grave."

"Who?" Thomas asked as a man wearing a baseball hat promoting the mosquito festival approached from the back room, inviting any last takers to join the poker game. Men only.

"So are the rest of us supposed to trade casserole recipes while we wait on the stronger sex? Too bad I forgot my tatting needles." Rose placed an entire fried shrimp in her mouth. "And Betty Friedan is only the woman who single-handedly..."

"I know who Betty Friedan is. I was only feeling nostalgic for you to explain her to me."

Rose ate another shrimp. Cocktail sauce dripped onto her wrist. As Thomas wiped it away, he remembered the anniversary bracelet. He removed the bracelet from his jacket. "Don't you think it's time you put this back on?"

"What is it?" Rose held the substantial piece of jewelry at arm's length. "No offense, but it's a little gaudier than I expected from someone like you."

"Gaudy?"

"Maybe I mean show-offy."

The waitress approached the table to refill Rose's water glass. The basket of fried food smelled strong long after Rose ate the final deep-fried mushroom. She asked the waitress for more napkins but turned down her offer of one more beer for the road.

After the waitress cleared their table, Rose said, "I like to make friends with people wherever I go. If I make friends, I will feel more intimate no matter where I end up in the world. A tour guide in a Moroccan souk even asked me once to be his assistant simply because..."

"You're lying."

"I am not!"

"You've never been to Morocco. You've never been anywhere but that one summer when you were fourteen and traveled with your American History class to that chocolate town in Pennsylvania and couldn't get over how the lampposts looked just like their famous chocolate Kisses."

"I still think someone in charge should have at least warned us about something so remarkable," Rose said, while another waitress ran a limp rag across their plastic tablecloth. "I mean, the person who designed those lamps captured every detail, down to the curves of the foil wrappings and the little white paper that pokes out the top of each candy like an invitation to open it up..."

"And peek inside," Thomas chimed in.

Rose stared at her lap long enough for a song on the jukebox to play right through. "I guess you really do know me."

Her new gold pony glinted beneath the bar lights as Thomas removed the charm from his pocket and attached it to his wife's bracelet. "How could I not? It's been ten years. Now stick out your arm."

Rose presented her right arm to Thomas. He tried to avoid catching any light brown down in the bracelet clasp. Once secured, the bracelet existed simply in its goldness, neither hiding nor showing itself off.

"I'm ready to go," Rose, still Rose, said as she stood from the table, the same moment glass panes on either side of the wooden front door bowed, but did not break, from the impact of an accident outside.

Taking a corner too fast to avoid an oncoming car—a car that could have easily held its own set of picnic sandwiches and nearly irreconcilable differences—a semi truck swerved into the side of the post office across the street. Thomas made a mental note to never buy his wife a golden cherry charm as the semi truck, upended, its driver lying near a still-spinning tire, released its cargo across the highway. Thousands of cherries bounced toward the bar like red-stemmed Ping-Pong balls.

"Come here, honey." Thomas pulled Rose to him. She smelled like warm lemons. Not a bad smell, but not Emma's smell. "Don't look."

She tried to squirm away as Thomas used the meat of his forearms to shield her from the accident. Even from across the street, he knew the truck driver had not survived. Rose fought harder as Thomas leaned in to give her a kiss. She turned her head. So much blood pooled across the asphalt. Without success he tried to kiss Rose again in an attempt to ignore his nausea.

In the moment it took Thomas to convince himself not to be sick—right there in front of all those strangers, the way a woman, not a man, would be sick after seeing something bad, the blood, the cherries like little harbingers of death, the imminent police sirens, then fire engines the same color—Rose broke free. In her bare feet, she ran out the front door of the bar toward the smoking truck. She ran through the aftermath of cherries without flinching as her feet smashed the fruit down to each knobby, hidden pit. She reached a body twisted into a lethal curve.

"Honey, don't touch him or you might catch something!" Thomas yelled after her. "Just wait with me until help comes."

He knew his wife would loosen the man's top button the way she once loosened Thomas's after a long day grading midterms. Every Friday night for a month, three or four years ago, Emma mixed Thomas a Manhattan before dinner. The couple's attempt to recapture the cocktail hour: the bourbon, the sweet vermouth, the shake of bitters. The floating cherry a bright red dot at the end of a sentence neither of them knew how to begin. Thomas knew Emma, now and forever Emma, would touch the man's face, try to breathe her air into him, give him the kiss of life with her honest mouth.

Emma rushed to perform CPR. From Thomas's viewpoint, his wife's actions looked more passionate than heroic, as if she were kissing a lover beneath the first early evening flickers of a small-town streetlamp surrounded by a bounty of ripe and undulating fruit. Whether his wife kept her lips pressed tight to the man's lips—breathing for him, pumping her crossed palms on his chest over and over until the rhythm of trying to save a stranger became as natural as the sound of her own breath catching in her lungs, her own heartbeat sped up but steady—or if she decided to turn and blow a kiss at her husband, an attempt at intimacy much too far away for Thomas to reach out and grab, a flash of gold reflected in the town's one streetlight caused Thomas to stop.

Emma's charm bracelet lay under his left foot, forgotten in the chaos of running toward a death neither one of them could reverse, or deny.

Best of Show

The postcards started arriving by late April, with pictures of half an ocean wave or the top third of a mountain peak.

"I like the cut of their jib," Tiny Ron said as he ran his petite fingers along the edge of each card. "Just look at the way this year's secretary wielded the paper cutter with mad skill. In the right light, I'd almost think this card was made for average-sized, run-of-the-mill assholes."

"Remember the year I trimmed so many postcards into fourths, you threatened to divorce me?"

"It was the sound of all the chopping getting to me, babe. It wasn't you."

My husband, the world's smallest man, seventeen and a half inches in stocking feet, jumped from his booster seat at the kitchen table. He held a stack of colorful correspondence the size of business cards in both hands as he landed on the counter, close to his lunch plate. Our agreement after the "rough patch" a few years ago began with Tiny Ron making most of his own meals. I've always hated cooking for a man, even before I quit my job as a journalist to run my husband's fan club.

Running a fan club is much less glamorous than the propaganda on TV, like Marcia Brady snagging Davy Jones to sing at senior prom. My day revolves around ordering headshots for my husband to sign with his trademarked minikin left thumbprint. I address and lick shut so many envelopes holding Tiny Ron's autographed photo that by night my head aches from the adhesive. Imagine how sexy a paper cut across the tongue feels married to the man who endorses those single-serving packets of Sriracha, which means whenever we eat out, I'm expected to cover all *my* food with it, too. You've seen the viral video starring Tiny Ron and Carrot Top? Each time the video gets a hit, my husband not only receives another like on Facebook, but another request for a photo, a speaking engagement, a movie pitch, a plea from someone at Make-A-Wish.

Everything felt so easy before social media invaded our lives. Back then, my husband and I fought like a normal couple about the way he folds clothes and the way I lack enthusiasm between the sheets. Now it's all Twitter updates and expanding his media platform, until spring rolls around each year and the postcards stack up like thin cakes on our foyer table, a table absent its legs so my husband can feel "normal in my own goddamn home!"

"Don't you think it's beneath you to work the fair circuit? Didn't Cruise promise you the part of Xenu's head alien once Weinstein greenlights the Scientology movie?"

We usually talk shop over dinner, a plate of leftover Kung Pao chicken for me, two black olives sliced on the bias and a shot glass–sized Manhattan for him. I've become expert, for those nights when I'm feeling charitable, at measuring Carpano Antica with a thimble and cutting a maraschino cherry into fourths with nail clippers before impaling a translucent red blob on a toothpick.

Some nights, I confess, I get my husband drunk to avoid sleeping with him. Maybe I'm not over the way things used to be, how he once pawed at my breasts like an angry cat or kicked my calves with his custom-made Docs. The biting I remember most of all. His mouth at my ankles, his rough tongue between my toes. But that was all before the counseling and the sobriety pledge required by a certain director of a certain space opera franchise.

"Babe, either I do the twelve steps or my legend becomes performing as an Oompa Loompa at a half-rate experimental theatre. They're turning a Vermicious Knid into the unreliable narrator. Fuck that."

On nights when I don't push another shot glass of whiskey, my husband and I either discuss business or he flirts until I allow him to enter my body with his inaudible grunts. I wouldn't say it's all bad, being married to a man small enough to carry around in a purse. He is handsome, his body a perfectly formed miniature version of everything women dream about. Hypopituitary dwarfism is like that. Some people in the business call this having the "Tom Thumb Blues," existing as a little man in a large world, the rarest of rare coins, diminutive but not proportioned the way we envision most Little People.

"I'll never get a strong troll roll looking like this. Forget anything having to do with *The Hobbit*."

On some nights, Tiny Ron does take my breath away. His taut abs, his firm biceps rippled in tattoos, a new favorite the phrase "Useless is the food that is fed to a satisfied person," in Sanskrit. A blanched tribal tattoo greens his other arm, his nineties souvenir of being carried, weightless, through the Lollapalooza crowds. It would be a lie to say his body posing before me at the foot of the bed doesn't stir me, much better than what I've taken to calling "life-sized" men, with their threatening strength and their cumbersome feet. When Tiny Ron undresses, then scuttles up the custom-built ladder to his side of the bed, I feel moisture rise between my legs. Tiny Ron is all man, but also all doll. The doll I can buy tea saucers to use as dinner plates. The doll I can order baby fedoras for online and silk Alexander McQueen handkerchiefs I've taught myself to sew into collared shirts. The doll I love, purring next to me in the dark, until the morning comes, and he turns over and speaks.

"So, babe, how will you ruin my day today?"

I could blame it on all the teasing. Maybe the hand-me-downs stripped off thrift-store dolls by his single mother through adolescence, or a general malaise brought about by the stars he was born under. Tiny Ron is not a pleasant man.

But then spring comes, our yearly reprieve. Those postcards. Our world, and our marriage, feel good, right, nearly romantic all the way through the final ride on the Scrambler before the closing of late August's last county fair.

Tiny Ron always sleeps with me the night the first postcard arrives. I wouldn't say it's the best sex I've ever had, and I don't even mind that anywhere he decides to place his tongue feels more like a buzzing little nuisance than a pleasure. I just want to feel close to him. I swear to God,

I don't even get annoyed when he stops in the middle of the act to discuss our upcoming fair circuit plans. Which one of the wives will drive the van this year, if it's strictly a kitsch thing, this low-country, hot-tented vaudeville. How someone should stop inviting Baby Liz because of her steady touring gig with Miley Cyrus. (This leaves Tiny Ron, Small Al, General Tom Thumb the Seventh, and Little Lucy.)

I push my husband's leg out from under the crushing force of my thigh. "But I want you to promise you'll stay away from Little Lucy. I know how much you like redheads."

"Don't worry, babe. Small Al told me in confidence that her drapes don't match her carpet."

We pack the way established couples pack, my suitcase and his suitcase open next to each other on our bed, both the same size, though Tiny Ron could zip himself inside without any contortion. He needs so many clothes for the tour, most of which I've sewn, along with the costumes for the other Little People Players. In what looks like a choreographed waltz, we lope back and forth from closet to dresser to suitcase, the seamless way married people go through each day, a vague, blurry notion of someone beside you in bed, fixing dinner in the kitchen, brushing their teeth, this entity, this force you live with but never really see because they are too close. Not too close emotionally or even psychically, but too close to the proximity of your reference point to step back and observe.

Tiny Ron never really sees me, though I am always there, buying his favorite olives, tugging out the slippery pimento so he can enjoy the brined fruit and the sweet pepper pieces in separate bites. I'm there to book his speaking gigs and cut the shortest pair of shoelaces in half and renegotiate his endorsement deals and shield him from overzealous fans who might accidentally crush him in their ardor. (The Star Wars dorks are the worst.) And I send out every new pair of skinny jeans to his favorite tailor. But I'm sure he still doesn't see me.

Maybe that's what love is: existing behind the scenes of another person's life.

I volunteer to drive the van on the first leg of the northwest tour. Late June and the heat seeps into me. The frizz overtakes my long, straight hair, hair I sometimes let my husband climb, even on tour, on the rare night I forget about the names he once called me and how I kept going back for more, surviving on the hope he would change with enough counseling and enough selective serotonin reuptake inhibitors cut into eighths, then twelfths.

Every year I forget to pack the right shampoo to rinse away the lingering scent of corn dogs. Antacids for too many curly fry dinners I mark in a ledger to write off on our taxes, though each season Little Lucy manages to sneak one or two red lipsticks into my box of receipts. I let it slip to keep peace in the community of average-sized partners and the Little People who love them.

Small Al's wife never travels in the van and never stays with us. She always rents a car and follows behind to control her music, her air conditioning, all the time ignoring the way her husband and Little Lucy sit together in the van's backseat, their chubby legs close. As I stare in the rearview mirror at the obvious summer romance, I can think only of linked Vienna sausages.

Little Lucy's boyfriend calls shotgun, which means for the rest of the tour I will drive with his average-sized profile on my right. When he and Little Lucy perform, he goes by Desi and wears a set of bongos on his chest, which looks like attachment parenting for musical instruments. Last year he told me his real name is Linden. I practiced saying his name in my head for the rest of the tour to block out the sounds of carnival riders paying to scream late into each night. Linden, Linden, Linden. A name to say out loud in bed. A name to be proud of when you introduce him as your husband, his average-sized hands made for pulling hair, not catching his too-small fingers in split ends. Last year, Linden and I got no closer than to share a funnel cake during a performance of Little Lucy singing "Umbrella" under a tent with a backing vocal that skipped, twice. No one in the audience seemed to notice that, or her dark roots.

You think someone married to the world's smallest man, whether or not he's handsome, would let her fantasies drift toward larger thighs, or stronger calves, or even a pronounced clavicle, but as Linden and I sat under the tent, our bodies trying to conceal our sweat, I felt most excited to eat a normal portion of food instead of going out to dinner with a man stuffed from one salad crouton.

With Linden up front and the rest of the crew in back—even General Tom Thumb the Seventh's little wife, on trial separation after he supposedly gave her HPV—we drive to our first stop. The Crook County Fair in central Oregon boasts its own rodeo arena, resident face painter, and baked goods competition, not to mention other contests for Best of Show in everything from sewing handmade dolls to making pen and pencil sets out of wood. The fair superintendent, impressed with our YouTube compilation video of last year's tour, rented us a cottage across the street from the fairgrounds. The little house offers more creature comfort than squeezing into a cramped camping tent, including a refrigerator stocked with single-serving pudding cups, both diet and regular. I hope, as we pull in and unload our things, that the hot tub off the back deck might afford me a chance to see Linden's torso. I haven't viewed a normal-sized male chest in years.

The troupe picks rooms. After a unanimous vote, they turn the hall linen closet into a practice space while I carry in more suitcases. Behind the louvered doors, Linden and I hear Little Lucy ask my husband in her mouse voice to take over the role of Desi.

"We haven't even unpacked yet and I'm already out of the show," Linden says. In the hot mid-afternoon, his profile looks like something carved out of ice cream. It doesn't matter what flavor. All I know is when I stare at him, I feel cooler.

Tiny Ron texts from the closet, "Can u call nearest music store for smallest set of bongos?"

I ignore him to study Linden's green eyes. Forcing myself to break his gaze and unpack takes most of my strength in the oppressive heat. I arrange the group's groceries. Fluff pillows. Make small talk with Tom Thumb and Small Al's wives before they decide to stay in a hotel room down the street. After they and their suitcases go, I try to settle in for a week of county fair living close to a man whose flip-flops, when he kicks them off next to the front door, take up more space than all of Tiny Ron's shoes arranged in a line.

Linden's shoes, they take up so much room. So do his T-shirts in the neat pile I fondle when he takes off for an afternoon jog around the neighborhood. I hold the shirts to my nose to inhale the scent of someone new, this foreign cotton settling against my lips, my lip gloss leaving a light pink ghost kiss someone with eyes as big as his will never notice. As I smell his clothes, even when I bury my face deep in the plastic lining of his suitcase, I think of my husband. How many plaid boxers could I sew from one of Linden's pairs? My husband creeps into each thought I try to hold tight about Linden, until Linden almost isn't there at all when I refold his shirts, when I hide the one with the lip print toward the bottom of the stack.

In the summer heat, the Little People Players rehearse their gnat whispers behind the closet doors. When I creep close, careful not to give away my presence, I hear General Tom Thumb the Seventh argue the merit of performing the coin flipping scene from *Rosencrantz and Guildenstern Are Dead*. Small Al, with his smoker's cough that always sounds like a sick cat, is on board. My husband argues against any Tom Stoppard play, at any time. His falsetto behind the closet door takes on an air of masculine power without any backbeat of coercion.

When I was sick once, the bad time we realized my body and his body weren't built to create a life strong enough to survive, me on the couch unable to erase what I saw in the middle of the night when I got up to pee and felt that warm, explicit carnage running down my thighs, Tiny Ron took care of me. He made me hot dogs and beans for supper. With a butter knife steady in both hands he sliced until the wiener resembled an octopus, which he displayed on top of the beans. From the Tupperware bowl marked PIMENTOS he placed two red peppers on the creature to mimic eyes. While I ate, my husband wove his small hand into my hair the way, I imagined, a baby's hand might grip my braid, if a baby was meant to be.

Tiny Ron held a garage sale the afternoon I went in for a final examination to clear me to try again. We never tried again. And I'll never know if my husband hired a company to pack up and move the crib and cotton candy bunting, or if the neighbors picked over the remains of our nursery. He shut and locked the door behind him and we never opened it. For months after, my husband pulled the pimento out of each olive himself.

Linden unlatches the back screen door. He jogs into the cramped living room smelling like an overdose of workout sweat mixed with fairground cut grass and a slight, disturbing undercurrent of barnyard. I like men who smell like men. On the living room couch, I thumb a copy of the Crook County Fair premium book. Canned peaches, spun yarn, a tooled leather belt, chiffon cake. Hundreds of opportunities to win Best of Show.

"Look at this." I show Linden the paper. His bulky body sinks the couch cushions when he sits close. "It reads like something from the fifties. A bunch of women baking cakes so a board can award ribbons. Painfully old-fashioned."

He grabs the booklet out of my hand. Tiny Ron's hands aren't big enough, can't grip tight enough, to grab anything away from anyone. The gesture feels domineering, dismissive in a way I'm not used to anymore.

"Why don't we enter?" Linden asks.

The sweat from his clunky palms dampens the booklet. Behind the closet door, Little Lucy practices "Dance Ten, Looks Three," which I protest every year as the show's finale until Small Al and Tiny Ron object and I end up sewing sequins on a teeny bikini so her large-assed little body can strut through the grass.

"Why not?" I say.

"All we have time to do at this point is bake something. I don't bake. Do you?"

I let my body relax next to his. "I've baked before, but nothing ever really took." Tiny Ron prefers to drink his dessert. Sometimes he even calls me his dessert.

Linden takes off his T-shirt like he's peeling a giant, ripe banana. I smell his sweat when he wipes his chest with the inside of the shirt. "Why don't we just buy a box of brownie mix and call it good?" he says.

His eyes. I realize how even his eyes look so large. Everything about this man is enormous, engorged, almost full of too much promise to corral into an affair.

"Hey, babe, what're you two up to?" Tiny Ron approaches in a tank top and Bermuda shorts I bought off a vintage Greg Brady doll. "We're all gonna hot tub now. Want to join us?"

I leave my answer up to Linden as he stands from the couch, bends down to show my husband the booklet, jokes about entering a dumb hick contest to keep us occupied before the fair opens.

"Sounds cool," Tiny Ron says. He asks for the sunscreen without looking up, his face even with the backs of my sun-burned knees. As I turn to look for the lotion in my bag, he kisses the back of one knee, soft and quick. "Let me know how it turns out."

Linden and I watch my husband frolic with Little Lucy on the back porch. Tiny Ron snaps a pic on his phone each time she rearranges her dyed red hair with the help of the hot tub water into a new style. Small Al and General Tom

Thumb take turns swimming laps through the jets of chlorinated water. Each year, the four of them together make me feel cumbersome in my own skin.

My focus becomes Little Lucy, with the little red braids and the little red mouth and the little red bikini. Linden discovers a brownie mix in the stocked pantry. He preheats without my help. Finds a bowl, two eggs, a cup for measuring water. Little Lucy's little mouth laughs too hard at my husband's jokes. Her little red fingernails, smaller than a row of Jelly Bellies, move too close to Tiny Ron's tattoos. Her little bikini inches up the crack of her fat ass as she springs from the water in what looks from the kitchen window like synchronized swimming.

"She's incorrigible," Linden says as we stand side by side, waiting for the smell of brownies to distract us, "but I don't think they've slept together. She prefers larger men. What do you prefer?" he asks. In a shocking movement, he places his hands around my waist and lifts me onto the counter next to the bowl coated in brownie batter. "Do you like feeling so small in my hands?"

He speaks too close to my face. A sour smell emanates from his pores. I like the smell of Tiny Ron's bourbon and his maraschino cherries, how he leaves nine-tenths of each cherry behind for me to slice in as many pieces as I feel like slicing, or not slicing at all, almost a full cherry to place in my own cocktail. I let Linden touch my face with his fingertips. Brownie batter sticks to my cheek before Linden licks my face, right there in the rented kitchen with the plaque of Jesus on the Cross prostrate above the refrigerator. And maybe it's what makes a couple a couple, or maybe it's what makes Tiny Ron my husband, but I know he saw us.

Maybe he smells, carried past the hot summer air mixed with bromine and brownie, the possible fertilization of one of my last viable eggs straining inside an ovary rejected by my husband's gametes. But he sees. The hot tub party ends as our oven timer beeps.

Linden removes the brownies from the oven a moment before I intend to push him away. I grab for a paper towel to wipe the invisible slime of his uninvited tongue from my face. Tiny Ron breezes past us in a cloud of watered-down Paco Rabanne, his wet little feet leaving prints across the dingy linoleum. Little Lucy follows, her prints a perfect match. From my spot, frozen on the kitchen counter, I hear the closet door shut with force, followed by Little Lucy running back to the hot tub. A sopping, crying little streak of discarded red.

Tiny Ron tosses beside me in bed. Throughout the mosquito-heavy night, I feel his toes, hot little nuggets, dig into my thighs. This is a first. I've never been able to make my husband jealous, and now he's too jealous of a normal-sized man snoring in the room next to us to dream his graphic Little Lucy dreams.

"Babe," he whispers around three in the morning, "why did you do it?"

I refuse to turn his direction. His toes knead me like unrelenting fingers. "I didn't do anything."

"But why'd you let yourself, you know." He burrows close to my back. For a moment I feel overly large, and for a moment he feels like an insect buzzing against me. "Why'd you let yourself notice such a large man?"

I don't have it in me, so late and with his toe prints tattooing me, to tell him I always notice larger men. I notice the large man at the grocery store who always comments on my demure appetite as he bags my Teddy Grahams next to my single-serving packets of cream cheese. I notice the dry cleaner and the mailman, the neighbor with one bad, though long, leg. The guy at the DMV who let me retake my license photo. Linden is just the latest man in a string of tall men I fantasize about unscrewing the tight lid off my peanut butter, embracing me with their extended arms in a way where I always have to look up.

"Linden's really not that much to notice," I say in the dark of our cottage bedroom. "It's not like he's a giant or anything."

It's not like I've imagined sex with a normal-sized man for over a decade, since my first interview with Tiny Ron during a Little People of America convention. It's not like Linden and I have plans to make love all over his room tomorrow morning after the Little People Players leave for dress rehearsal. It's not like I can hardly sleep, with all the oversized anticipation beating against the chamber of what's starting to feel like my very, very large heart.

I sneak into Linden's room early in the morning after the troupe share a collective bagel and head to the fairgrounds. The air still smells of Little Lucy's overly sweet drugstore perfume, but their bed looks untouched, Linden asleep on top of the country chic duvet.

"I've been waiting for you," he says as I shut the door. I inch my way toward his body. He smells like the warmth of sleep as his arms pull me onto his chest in a move almost terrifying in its swiftness.

"Why me?" I whisper like a shy girl.

"Why not?" he answers.

Before I have much time to think he removes my pajamas, is in me, my body not ready for his body, my body stretched and hurting, then he's out of me and done. Just like Tiny Ron. Just like most men before him. Linden falls back asleep on top of the bed. I gather my clothes and leave his room without shutting the door. When I glance back, it's like I was never even there.

The morning waltzes into another hot afternoon as my two-minute affair recedes from my mind. I roam the small, paneled hallway of our rental feeling like a creature too large for my knick-knacked cage. Linden gets up to go jogging. We pass each other in the hall. He doesn't look at me.

"Is something wrong?" I question the back of his T-shirt.

At the front door he says, "Have you heard from those guys?"

"I haven't."

"Cool!" he yells. He slams the screen door. I hear the sound of his large tennis shoes pushing away big swaths of gravel as he sprints down the driveway.

The Crook County Fair premium book clearly states that exhibitors are to turn in six individual brownies for judging in the brownie category. In the kitchen, I look for the pan of brownies on each of four counters laden with Lord's Prayer spoon rests and wooden banana holders. When I peer into the sink, full of dirty dishes from the night before, resting on top of the pile I find the empty, crumby pan.

It won't change anything to ask whether Linden devoured the plate last night after I went to bed, or Little

Lucy sabotaged my chance at being good at something besides being a famous man's wife.

I wander the fairgrounds past the lines of excited bakers checking in their goods. My envy unloads over the exhibition hall as I scan the card tables weighted in pies and cookies and cakes. Beyond the baked goods area, I walk by quilts with seams almost too small to see. The sewing competition catches my attention even more than a local woman in the brownie line, whose brownies don't look nearly as delicious as mine once looked. As ours once looked, mine and Linden's, my foolish attempt to create something important and memorable with a handsome man I hardly know.

The sewing and handicrafts area looks like something out of one of my mother's old Butterick pattern books, so many afghans and sundresses. Then I see the Fashion Doll table. That's what the Crook County Fair calls the category, Fashion Dolls translating to clothes hand-sewn for dolls the exact size of Tiny Ron. I'm tempted to take pictures of a doll wearing a suit only half as accurately tailored as my husband's three-piece ensemble. I even know how to crease a fourth of a cut and serged pocket square into a precise presidential fold. Mentally scanning the contents of Tiny Ron's suitcase, I feel confident several outfits could win a ribbon. Maybe the Armani jeans I scaled down, paired with a Louis Vuitton belt I tooled from the broken strap of a handbag Tiny Ron bought me years ago with a very small part of his *Willy Wonka and the Chocolate Factory* head Oompa Loompa royalty check. On my particularly long mend after the miscarriage, I attempted to copy an

Alexander McQueen coat that belonged to Ronnie Wood. We had taken pictures of the real coat on an anniversary trip to Lake Tahoe's Hard Rock Casino. Now my husband never travels without what he calls his "magic coat."

How can I get the clothes checked in before the cutoff time to submit exhibits? How will I find dolls the correct size to model a trousseau of miniature haute couture in this small town?

"Hey, babe, what are you doing in here?" On a practice break, Tiny Ron spots me gazing longingly at the fashion dolls. "Did you enter your brownies?"

I worry about the pink of his skin, how his older tattoos almost disappear into a sunburn. "How'd you know I was in here? And, no, I didn't have anything to turn in."

"I was looking for you. What are you fucking talking about, nothing to turn in?"

"It just didn't seem very important when I woke up today, is all."

Tiny Ron hops onto the table next to the fashion dolls in an attempt to make me laugh. He does his version of the two-step before posing next to a boy doll draped in some sort of poorly made *Game of Thrones* costume. "Of course it's important, kiddo. If it's important to you, it's important to me."

"But somebody either threw them out or ate them." As much as I want to stop myself, I start to cry, right in front of the Fashion Doll table. "And why don't any of you like me, because I know none of you really do. I drive you around everywhere and I unpack everything and I shop for single-serving cups of applesauce, and I even leave you alone to sleep with whomever you want. Why isn't that enough, for all of you?"

I turn and run from the exhibition hall.

* * *

Opening day of the fair arrives with a voice from the crackling loudspeaker announcing the afternoon debut of the Little People Players. I walk from the cottage to the main entrance alone. A flash of my backstage entertainer badge and I'm in, free admission. I take my time and visit every chicken in the poultry barn. The exotic breed with what look like feathered leg warmers frightens me. I learn later that guinea pigs are also called cavies. I guess how many black-eyed peas it takes to fill a Mason jar. Outside the main fair tent, two smaller white tents display a plastic fetus to represent each month of development in utero. There are tents next to these tents selling vacation time-shares and scarves to freeze and wear around your neck and hippie crystals and even hot tubs.

Hours pass, the fair sweeping me up in its sweet nostalgia as I wander past more chickens and rabbits and 4-H displays, midway games, carnival rides. I treat myself to an elephant ear. The Little People Players debut show of this fair season comes and goes. From the corner of my eye, I can see a flash of dyed red hair prance around the main stage and another flash of Tiny Ron's sunburned face much too close to a tiny red bikini top.

With a hot dog in one hand and a soda in the other, I walk from the main row of tents toward a small tent pitched alone under a tree. A sign at the front entrance of the circus-striped canvas says in ornate calligraphy, "Come Inside and Meet The World's Most Unusual Thing." A man waits at the entrance. A normal-sized man, neither handsome nor ugly; a man without need for a fan club or a backstage rider that includes someone picking out all of the green M&M's.

"For a dollar," the man sizes me up, then tells me, "you can step inside and meet The World's Most Unusual Thing." A flap covers the main tent. Through a slit in what looks like a shower curtain, a green light glows like the glow of something primordial. "Is it the cousin of the Fiji Mermaid? Perhaps the unholy offspring of the Jersey Devil and El Chupacabra? I dare you to come in and take a peek."

"Believe me, I'd be tempted if I wasn't already married to Tiny Ron." I finish my hot dog. The man throws away my mustard-stained napkins without me having to ask.

"Tiny Ron from the movies? I love that guy. Isn't he the one in those hilarious commercials? And wasn't he on *Celebrity Big Brother* a few years ago?"

"It's not at all what you'd think, living with the world's smallest man. And before you ask," I say between long sips of watered-down soda, "yes, the sex is pretty normal, and no, we don't have it any more than anyone else. And yes, he's in those commercials, and yes, he was on *Big Brother*. He would've won, too, if he hadn't acted like such an ass at the very end of the season. And trust me, nothing in your tent will ever be more unusual than being married to him."

"Very good, very good," the man says. He pulls a pink ticket off a large roll. "Use this later if you want to get into my show, no charge. You never know what you might find."

"Me and The World's Most Unusual Thing." I hold the ticket safe in my moist palms. "Thanks, I'll be sure to come back," I say the way women who plan on never returning always do.

Before I call it a day, and the fair closes, I check out the exhibit hall a final time. Every winning pie has its blue ribbon. The cakes, too. No brownies won anything but dark green participant ribbons that curl down each paper plate like something reptilian.

I can't help but be drawn back to the sewing area, and to the fashion dolls. A doll with Bermuda shorts wears a second-place, lipstick-red ribbon. First goes to what looks like a baby prom dress. I sense someone watching me as I examine each doll in the row.

Glancing around, I see nothing until the Best of Show ribbon catches my attention, with its long coil of rainbow satin culminating in a rainbow rosette. It's on Tiny Ron's magic coat! I recognize the color and cut. Then I see my husband, posed in one of the best pieces I have ever made, Best of Show ribbon pinned to his slight, yet proud, chest. He stands looking straight ahead with both hands on his hips.

"Look, doll, you did it!" He points to the ribbon as I stare, confused by why he's on the Fashion Doll table and how he entered my coat in the competition. "Who needs brownies when you can do this?"

Tiny Ron unpins the ribbon from his chest. From his high perch on the table, he bends to hand the ribbon to me in a gesture that reminds me of a knight's coronation. My other hand holds the little pink ticket, a future admission to something maybe even more unusual than being married to the world's smallest man. I turn the ticket over and over in my normal-sized hand.

Reducing

They called it *reducing*. A bastardized colloquialism lost in translation by the woman who made the morning talk show rounds hocking her book about French women who never got fat. Veronica had read the book three times, a luxury afforded during slow moments at her museum docent job. She also had time to read the book three times because her mother was just rich enough to pay her rent and just thin enough to encourage Veronica to whittle her body into a shape a little more svelte.

Veronica's mother enjoyed calling everything without a noticeable shape "svelte." Each winter she said, "Oh, Veronica, look at the svelte aspen trees. Aren't they lovely this time of year?" Or, "I hope they don't recreate those svelte buildings for the World Trade Center memorial." Or even, "I miss the old rotary dial phone I grew up with, the anticipation of waiting for the dial to click back to zero before my call went through, and that phone cord that curved around my svelte waist. That was back in the day when everyone loved Susan Anton. Did you ever see that one movie where she unapologetically towered her svelte frame over her leading man? That would've never happened in your grandmother's time, what with everyone worshipping pudgy little Marilyn Monroe."

"Mom!"

"Well, I'm surprised she didn't crash clean through that grate, with her chunky legs. She puts on that white dress and everyone goes crazy for her with no concern that she probably has a thyroid problem, at the very least."

Veronica and her mother talked mostly about being svelte, celebrities and their botched plastic surgeries, and how gratuitous a gesture it was that Starbucks announced the calories of every dessert.

"Isn't it a pity corporate headquarters felt the need to share the most gruesome details?" her mother asked as she and Veronica removed a birthday cake–flavored cake pop from its white stick before dissecting it with the skill of a surgeon trained to operate on miniatures.

The two women cut the round ball in half. They kept halving the halves until they were left with tiny pink confections the size of flakes of confetti.

Her mother said, "What will Roger think of you splurging like this? Naughty us."

Veronica's mother had a way of injecting herself not only into Veronica's body image, but into her relationships. Veronica had vowed not to over-share this new man. Every other short-lived relationship got pulled through what Veronica referred to as "The Wringer," a ritual of one shared cake pop between two women as her mother prodded and dutiful Veronica, gumming each morsel into a sticky froth, supplied.

Roger was not Wringer material. In a downtown gallery he curated pottery from ancient places Veronica pretended to know about. He wore unfashionable glasses and took two homemade sandwiches for lunch. More than anything, Roger was off-limits because he called Veronica "Ronnie" and no one, not even her father on their father-daughter dinner dates when she was still young enough to not comprehend the calories in an ice cream sundae, had ever called her that. And Roger was fat. Veronica had never gone out with a fat man before.

"Let's go to the movies, Ronnie," Roger said.

He didn't ask why she only pretended to eat her popcorn before bumping into her own elbow to spill the buttery mess on the theater floor. He didn't ask why Veronica, Ronnie to him, sipped from her Diet Coke instead of slurping down to the free refill line.

He didn't even ask why Veronica whispered, right before the first preview, "If I hold onto your arm halfway through, it's only because I might float away."

The movie centered around a family who set up residence in an obviously haunted house: husband whose car only starts when no one is in it, wife whose dishes disorganize themselves during the night, a little girl who talks to her invisible playmate, a cat who runs away. Veronica's breath sped up during each scene, but not because of the possibility that a portal to Hell hid in the family's basement.

She was reducing.

If Veronica could only train her body to slim those hips another inch and suck in an imperceptible gut...at a hundred and four and a half pounds, Veronica needed to reduce two more pounds to feel svelte. The more she dreamed about losing weight, the tighter she held onto Roger, her three-date boyfriend.

"Oh, Ronnie, don't be afraid. It's just a movie," he said as she closed her eyes and clawed the sleeve of his XXL black T-shirt. "At least one of these hapless dimwits will survive so they can make a sequel," he whispered, unconcerned with the moviegoers clustered around them.

"If I don't hold on tight, I'll float all the way up to the ceiling before I finally disappear."

Veronica's hunger made her words sound slow and far away. Words going down the waterspout like the itsy bitsy spider. Over the movie projector's perpetual click-clack, she heard her heart beating between her ears. She wanted to eat her dropped popcorn off the dirty floor. She wanted to follow this with hot turkey sandwiches piled in mashed potato fluff. She wanted to be able to eat a normal dinner without hating herself afterward. She wanted Roger to cook lasagna for her, layered with full-fat cheese. Most of all, she wanted Roger to quit talking. Her nails grazed his skin.

"Just focus on the character you think will make it to part two and you won't be so afraid," he said.

Since the couple sat in a theatre and there was no way, even with a high ceiling, that she could float out into space, Veronica wasn't afraid of anything but her overwhelming desire to eat food off the movie theater floor. Just one forgotten Whopper, just one misplaced popcorn kernel. If she had seen a candy rolling around on the floor, she would have placed it in her mouth without apology. She knew she was close to falling in love with Roger because of the way she forgot to lie to him. She'd already confessed how she sometimes went for days without eating, and other times how she baked double or triple brownie batches, devouring them until her head throbbed.

"Am I floating away yet?" she asked as the movie credits rolled.

Veronica never opened her eyes to see which family member survived. She hoped in the fuzzy background of her brain that the cat used up only one life. Roger probably assumed his almost girlfriend's talk of floating was a new kind of female sexual code unknown to the online dating world, those insular emails leading nowhere but the ubiquitous string of first dates with few second helpings.

"No, Ronnie, you aren't floating away yet, but you will be very soon."

"Is it time for pie?" She stood to stretch away two hours of sitting in the dark instead of making out.

Veronica thought all men wanted to touch her because all men wanted to touch everything from boyhood on: those little toy cars, bugs, bicycle chains, the motors of bigger and bigger cars. Of her seven first dates in the last few months since putting up her Internet profile, Veronica faked seven orgasms in three different movie theaters. Internet profiles attracted the kind of men who chose companions, even temporary ones, from a series of posed photos that tried to look spontaneous. To Veronica the whole thing felt like selecting a mail-order bride for the night.

She stopped eating two days before each first date to

ensure the proper tingle along her nerves without actually bumping her weightless body against the lush, folded fabric of the theatre ceiling. She wore the same crotchless stockings and tastefully short black skirt. She guided each of seven unfamiliar hands toward her body, most of the time before the previews ended. If the theater was empty enough to sit in the back row, the men sometimes stroked themselves while they touched her. Others gasped as their tentative fingers skimmed the demarcation line between her lower stomach and pubic hair. One or two just went for it, fast and rough. Veronica tried not to cringe as her body made contact with a jagged hangnail.

Keeping her eyes closed the whole time helped Veronica bask in the sensation of floating. Sometimes, if one of the men's fingers brought her close enough to dissolve into her body's pleasure, she denied herself this pleasure, punished herself for being on a date with a man who would touch her before the movie even started. She would buck and whinny in phony gratification until the men removed their hands.

When she accepted Roger's first date request, she had already seen the same movie with a different man. As the opening credits flashed, she moved Roger's thick hand between her legs.

He stopped her before he breached her seductive clothes, which her mother had said, over a shared cake pop, made her look "whorish but svelte."

"My goal tonight," Roger whispered in the dark, "is to really get to know you. I hope you want to get to know me, too. Why rush to the end when we don't even know which race we're in?"

Veronica spent the entire movie focused on its plot instead of honing her sexual acting skills. After the movie,

Roger took her for coffee and pie at a diner in the arts district downtown, close to where he worked. As the pie arrived, its downy meringue enveloping a neon lemon filling, Veronica wondered how it felt to size up pottery all day. How did one vase make the cut when a bowl didn't? Did Roger randomly choose a certain piece because he liked its color, its shape, its provenance, or did he run out of time at a specific point each afternoon and pick what sat before him? Was that the same way, Veronica wondered, he'd selected her from the dating site they both subscribed to: two single professionals who ran in the same canapé fundraiser circles, but had yet to curate each other?

Three dates later, Veronica was almost ready for Roger to take her to his house. Of course he had his own private pottery collection. She liked the idea of being surrounded by so many priceless, breakable things in the house of an extra-large man. Maybe, lying beneath him in bed, Veronica would feel small. She longed to feel small almost as much as she longed to disappear.

First came the ritual of coffee and pie, seated at opposite sides of a diner banquette. Veronica's narrow body barely indented the faux leather. The booth creaked under Roger's heavyset frame.

"Look how different we both are," he said.

Veronica examined the pie menu. Imagine that, a restaurant with a menu devoted to pie. Not a small and sticky dessert menu, or even a pie and sundae menu. Just pie. Twenty-four flavors with the franchised trademark of a different pie for every hour in the diner's twenty-four-hour day.

"How are we different?" Veronica pretended to listen while she focused on what looked like a nearly animatronic photograph of a coconut cream pie.

"Well, for one thing, we've seen three different movies in the past three weeks, but I get the sense you don't even like movies."

"You're right. I don't."

"And we've faithfully come here after each show, but I don't think you like pie much, either."

The more Roger studied Veronica under the diner's florescence, the more she imagined devouring the coconut cream. She wanted to eat enough pie to make her feel sick, but not too much that it prevented her from floating away, especially in an emergency.

"You are very wrong about that one," she said, hoping no one would notice as she slipped the laminated pie menu into her purse. "I adore pie. It's just that right now I'm reducing."

"I know enough about women to know that's some fake French term for dieting."

"Correction. It's real French, not fake. I've read the book."

"No, more like it's ridiculous. You're a person who in no sense of the word needs to reduce. In fact, it's just the opposite. I think you could actually stand to gain."

"Please don't ruin this," she said, as the waitress approached their table.

Right in front of a blonde with "Bridget" stamped on her plastic nametag, though Veronica guessed the waitress's real name to be something much more un-svelte, Roger said, "We won't be ordering tonight."

"Roger, please."

"My date doesn't eat. The most lovely woman I've met refuses to even share a piece of pie with her very interested beau."

from her purse and tossed it in the bathroom trash.

Veronica reapplied her lipstick in the mirror. She struggled to find her lips as her form seemed to fade in and out. Was this what one calls a loss of sentience? One hand held tight to the garrote she knotted with her purse strings and brush handle. She texted Roger with her free thumb.

Her first text said:

I'm only apologizing to you because I'll
be leaving here soon.

> You don't have to apologize. And you
> didn't have to call a cab. I'd still be happy
> to drive you home.

I didn't call a cab. I'm not going home.

> You're not?

Where I'm going, only other thin women
will be able to find me.

> Oh, Ronnie, you don't mean like Karen
> Carpenter thin, right?

Don't be crass. I'm being serious. I'm
almost ready. But I didn't want to leave
without telling you.

> Well thanks for that, I guess.

Don't mention it.

                              Can I come into the bathroom
                              and talk to you, face to face?

You can try.
But you won't be able to see me.

                              But will you still let me try?

Sure. And if you show up,
please bring pie.

It took a few minutes for Roger to order all the pies he
thought might please his girlfriend. He didn't care what Veronica thought, and called her his girlfriend to anyone who
would listen, even though she'd twice told him not to. She en-
deared herself to him by the way she never mentioned how
he had to hook his belt buckle on the side of his body, right
above his hip, because his gut stuck out too much to wear it in
its proper place. He liked how her thinness never seemed to
amplify his fatness. Most of all, he liked how people in public stared at them like they were somehow miraculous, this
beautiful, lithe creature and the cumbersome man beside her.

Roger asked the waitress for the pies to go, one slice
each of four flavors. Ronnie wasn't the kind of woman who
liked apple—too provincial, he thought—so he opted for
exotic flavors. Rum raisin, peaches and cream, smores,
kiwi lime. He carried four small to-go boxes into the bathroom, aware of the deviance he felt carrying food across
the threshold into a slightly unsavory public place.

"Ronnie?" he yelled to alert any unsuspecting women of the domestic bump in the road he felt certain eating pie could fix. "Is anyone else in here with you?"

Standing before the mirror in a woman's restroom felt no different than standing before the mirror in a men's restroom. He set the boxes of pie on the counter, wet from what looked like frequent and aggressive hand washing, and called out to Ronnie again.

A woman's voice from behind a stall answered, "I think your date left. She told me to give this to the man who came looking for her."

Over the stall door the woman handed him Veronica's purse, its leather strap broken off on one side. Roger turned the purse over and over in his hands. He fingered the knots, a complicated weapon or weight his girlfriend had designed and tied in the time it takes most women to double-check their hair in a mirror.

"Excuse me, did she say anything else to you?"

"Yes." Roger heard the toilet flush behind the stall. "Your girlfriend told me to tell you that she tried to anchor herself to you, somehow, but it didn't work. And then she tried anchoring herself to her purse strap, but that didn't work, either. And that she hoped the pie would make you feel better."

"Veronica actually thought some shitty diner pie could make me feel better about being dumped?"

Roger sensed the woman wouldn't come out of the stall until he left the bathroom. He stared at his reflection in the mirror, pretended to wash his hands until the woman behind the stall made a quick exit past him. Something about staring at his overweight reflection in a woman's bathroom made him feel a combination of shame and excitement.

In a new ritual belonging only to him, Roger opened each small white box to examine the pieces of pie. Offerings to a woman who didn't love him quite yet, but there was power in his longing to accept Veronica and to understand her. There was power, most of all, in his longing to belong to her.

Roger abandoned the four flawless pieces of pie on the bathroom counter, no matter how much his stomach ached from skipping dinner. He felt lighter with each step out the bathroom door and down the diner's dingy hallway.

"So this is how it feels to reduce," he said to himself as he stood, alone, in the middle of the parking lot. "Soon, I just might float away."

Roger scanned the sky for Veronica—up there, somewhere just past his sight, holding onto a cloud, waiting.

The Line of Fate

With her teeth, Tabitha tore the sutures from the middle finger of her left-hand ostrich glove in the Nordstrom's bathroom. Nubby sections of dyed red leather pulled away from each other like a bad cut. The flesh of her middle finger, manicured tip golden as the newest winter makeup trend, darkened when she ran cold water over the exposed flesh.

"This is almost like getting a new finger," she said to the bathroom mirror. "One step closer to a better hand."

Holiday music jazzed its sugarplums through the speakers. The air smelled like cinnamon. Under the bathroom florescence, her finger looked alien thrust through the surface of so much cold weather gear. From her wooly beret to her snow boots, Tabitha had shrouded her body against the Pacific Northwest's endless winter to brave the department store crowds.

Black velveteen, a green plaid wool blend, now the red Ostrich—in the weeks since Halloween and the first appearance of storm clouds descending over the city, Tabitha had chewed through three pair of gloves. Always in the bathroom at Nordstrom's, always in front of a curved, water-splattered mirror, now with a chorus of piped-in music Santa Babying her onward.

"Santa Baby, I've been an awful good girl," she purred toward her cloudy reflection. "Though it's funny to call myself a girl, isn't it?"

Other women squirted holiday-scented hand sanitizer onto their palms, emergency travel-sized Bath and Body backup, to avoid the bay of sinks too near the woman ripping at her leather. The women never got close enough to realize Tabitha was only pretending. Not to devour the most expensive gloves the city offered, but to break through those gloves with new hands. Each time, for the few moments it took her well-moisturized, well-tended skin to surface, she could pretend she was cataloging the hand of a stranger. Something foreign in its dimensions, smooth as the fired bisque of the patients she once helped mend at the doll hospital in her mother's basement.

After Tabitha's father died, her mother, the town seamstress in a time when people fixed clothes instead of throwing them out, ran a doll hospital for extra income. For hours every night, Tabitha sat across from her at a card table under the glare of harsh basement lighting. Her mother mended frayed bows or set fallen, synthetic curls before gluing back together a shattered face or broken pelvis, the common emergency crisis of children over-loving their doll companions into an early grave.

An amateur astrologist, Tabitha's mother made up stories for each doll she repaired among the sewing bric-a-brac. Baby Doll, the one belonging to the neighbor girl who always combed her hair so hard, the plastic doll fibers almost fused together, was obviously born under the sign of Taurus.

"How do you know that?" Tabitha asked. She clutched her Raggedy Ann doll tight to her chest. With a free hand, she reached her stubby fingers toward the newest specimen, but never touched. Those were the rules.

"This doll was born under the sign of Taurus, just like you, Tabby, because she is obstinate."

"Obstinate?"

The smell of doll hair hung sickly sweet in the small room.

"Stubborn. Steadfast. Loyal to a fault." Her mother held up the blonde mess of hair toward her daughter's face. "Look how she takes such abuse."

Just this one time, the child stuck her small pinky finger deep inside the newly formed curl her mother had worked from a tangle into a ringlet. The yellow hair wrapped around her finger the way a baby grabs hold of a grown-up's much larger hand.

Her mother asked, "Do you know why Baby Doll will be okay?"

"Because she has such pretty hair?" Tabitha released her finger the second she said this, afraid of giving preferential treatment to some stranger's companion over Raggedy Ann and her fuzzy bouffant of red yarn.

"Because no one's marred her hands. Look at her beautiful little hands. Hands, my girl, are the real windows of the soul."

Tabitha set Raggedy Ann on the table. Bending her head almost close enough to touch her lips to Baby Doll's fingers, she examined the doll's little white hands. Bone white. Teacup white. Reaching the middle of a Creamsicle on a summer day white, with light pink fingernails almost too tiny to see, and palms smooth as eggshell, with just the slightest indentation of a line.

"Do you know that dolls can always be fixed, no matter how cracked or beaten or broken? It's because of their Line of Fate. Their hands have been blessed with an eternal pleasant outcome, a happy destiny. Wish we could all be so lucky. Now look, here's Violet Doll. Her owner really seems to enjoy eating honey. And here's Sunny Doll, a trooper to the end. Definitely a Virgo. So conscientious all the time."

Her mother's words floated away from Tabitha as she studied the palms of each of the dolls lying in decidedly unladylike heaps on the card table. More than anything Tabitha wanted to reinvent her palms. Even as a child, Tabitha longed for a clean slate. In her head she called it a do-over, and the thin book on fortune telling in her school's library confirmed her suspicions.

Other mothers had tried to ban the volume, one in a set of slumber party game books that detailed, with cartoon images, everything from how to apply eye shadow to how to throw a make-your-own pizza party. The book, really a junior high read the younger girls salivated over, contained an entire section on fortune telling. Every genre of what the League of Christian Mothers deemed the Dark Arts was represented: reading tea leaves, fortune telling with a crystal ball, tarot cards. What interested Tabitha most was a diagram of a palm. She spent hours studying the pen and ink drawing that covered the page like half of an insistent clap.

One day, Tabitha brought the book home, and her mother pointed out the Heart Line, Head Line, Life Line, and the Line of Fate. After studying the diagrams, Tabitha still could not differentiate the scratches etched along her own palms.

"See, right here." Tabitha's mother gripped one of her daughter's hands, hard. She scratched her long fingernails over Tabitha's ticklish palm. "Heart Line, Head Line, Life Line." Her mother leaned closer. "I don't see your Line of Fate anywhere. How odd. Why, in all my years, I don't think I've ever seen a little girl, and definitely not a little doll, without one."

Maybe this meant Tabitha was born cursed. That her Line of Fate, no matter how much she moisturized and manicured was, somehow, eternally invisible, eternally broken.

Once she graduated past slumber party books, the words getting longer, the diagrams progressing in detail, Tabitha sought out professional psychics. The money spent on what her first, second, third (and current) husband called utter frivolity could keep the psychics in tarot cards for decades.

The thing about psychics, Tabitha thought as the cinnamon air of the Nordstrom's bathroom spiced around her exposed finger, was that each one told her something entirely different.

"I'm sick of it. Who cares whether or not someone can read my future. What I need is to change my destiny," she said to the mirror, "and everyone knows there's only one way to do that." Tabitha turned to the mirrored likeness of another shopper. "Excuse me?"

The shopper washed her hands in the next sink over without shying away from the woman who chewed on her own gloves. "Me?" the woman asked.

Tabitha hated that the woman knew how to wear a ribbon in her hair. "Do you know if there's a Chinatown around here?"

"It's nowhere near the size of the one in San Francisco, but it's big enough to find lunch and tea, I think." The woman wrote directions on a paper towel. She nudged the towel toward Tabitha's intact, gloved hand.

"Do you think they'll mind my silly gloves?" Tabitha asked.

"They probably won't even notice."

Tabitha looked up from the handbag snug in the crook of her right arm. "Oh I'm sorry," she said to the woman, "I was talking to my doll."

The woman scurried toward the bathroom door. Tabitha placed the ripped red glove finger in her pocket.

Chinatown comprised two streets that ran parallel to each other, with two smaller streets cut through the middle. Decades ago, city planners had replaced the street lamps with red lampposts wrapped in yellow metal dragons, which bared their fangs at the top of each light.

"This place almost looks magical. We've got to be able to find our answers somewhere near here," she said to her purse. The doll did not answer as Tabitha studied a map torn from a free local paper. Ducks hung by their roasted necks in grease-smeared windows. A row of identical stores sold silk Mary Janes with brown rubber bottoms. "Wouldn't you look cute in a pair of those?" she teased.

Tabitha knew to stop walking when all of the store signs, and then even the street signs, changed to logograms. How could she explain what she wanted to an herbalist, anyway?

She imagined herbalists to be more like ancient apothecaries, dispensing spiced medicines suspended in drops of hardened sugar. One of her friends swore by the poultice an herbalist in Seattle said improved fertility. Another touted ginseng tea as the cure to her sugar addiction, but made all her friends swear never to post her secret on Facebook.

Tabitha didn't need a poultice to cure anything or a potion to find love or even a magic spell for good fortune. Her body never ached, she only ate candy when she was on her period, her husband loved her enough, and made more than enough money for her to add to her doll collection every other week. She was the rare kind of person who believed she was living a good, genuine life. Only her life belonged to someone else.

Tabitha was born with the wrong Line of Fate. Sometimes this happened, a psychic told her years ago. Did your mother induce labor? Was your father in the Navy? Did your parents celebrate Valentine's Day? All these random bits of flotsam, harmless occurrences mixed with facts that make a life, can sometimes add up to a person being born with the wrong palms.

The psychic quickly corrected herself as Tabitha held her purse tight and scanned for the exit. "There's nothing to be afraid of. It's not always like you're walking around with a specific person's life plan instead of your own, though it has been known to happen. It's more likely your palm lines are a little out of focus, blurred at the edges. Someone in charge drafted the blueprint of your destiny one size too small to contain all your deepest dreams."

"But I don't even remember my dreams," Tabitha said.

"Exactly," the psychic answered.

She showed Tabitha a brochure, glossy and tri-folded, of options to change the course of her destiny. This menu of incantations contained the exact price the psychic charged, plus tax and gratuity, next to each intended outcome.

As Tabitha stood in front of the herbalist's door, she forgot which spells she had asked the psychic to concoct for her. She had seen so many psychics and read so many of their brochures that her memories smudged around their perimeters, much like the Line of Fate on her palms. Whatever amount she paid, plus gratuity, had not altered anything.

Dolls couldn't really be the superior beings, could they? One tumble off a high shelf and even her mother couldn't make a doll whole again. Tabitha loved it when a customer brought a companion too far gone, a Humpty Dumpty of the doll world whose Line of Fate had shattered beyond mending.

A bell jingled as she entered the herbalist's shop. The man at the front counter looked up from a Chinese soap opera playing on a small television.

"You are in the wrong store," the man said.

"But I was told?"

The man raised the television's volume. He turned to speak to Tabitha over the romantic melee. "We have nothing for you here. Your problem is much more serious than too many cigarettes or cream puffs or the fact that you always carry a doll around in your purse."

Her heart dashed around beneath her skin. Tabitha caressed the inside of her coat pocket, attempted to locate the finger of her torn glove as if this man could see not only through her body to the soul beneath, but inside her designer handbag and the lined pockets of her expensive wool. She had left a trail of torn gloves all over town. Her husband would probably commit her if he ever saw the abused finger sheaths scattered like tongues in city parks close to their condo, so many found objects for an artist to place in a diary or a child to collect in a keepsake box or even a group of teenage boys to make sexual jokes about. She wanted to throw the red finger at the man, but shook too hard to grasp the flaccid leather.

Tabitha said, "What you're doing is some sort of racial profiling. I've seen stories about this on Dateline, but never in a million years thought they were true."

Again the herbalist raised the volume knob on the television. On the soap, a man and woman argued about something while they stood in a living room. He paced, she clutched her hands, a man in the next room pressed his ear to the wall. Tabitha was surprised Chinese people sat on the same kind of couch as American people, that they decorated with coordinated lamps and matching side tables.

"If you think I'm just another rich bitch looking for herbs to lose weight, you're very wrong. And how do you know there's a doll in my purse?" Tabitha directed her question to the man but stood transfixed by the television, the *in flagrante delicto* the Chinese soap star heard through the wall, all the ensuing tragedy.

She forced her eyes away from the set. "Whether or not I am supposed to say so, I'm not seeing any of the 'Chinese magic' in here we white people have heard about since birth."

"See how you never remove your gloves, even inside? You were born with the wrong hands," the man said. "The only thing left to do is to cut them off." He turned the volume on his television so high, Tabitha heard a palpable static arc between the two lovers. The actor on the other side of the wall seemed unaffected.

"Either you're really sick, or we're experiencing a deep cultural divide."

The torn leather finger lounged in Tabitha's coat pocket. She now felt positive the herbalist knew about the severed finger, guessed at the sharpness of her incisors and the largeness of her bank account.

The man said, "You need to find the person who has your hands. She will need to cut hers off, too. Then you exchange and everyone is happy."

Tabitha turned to leave the store.

"And here." The man handed her a small pocketknife. He pointed to Tabitha's handbag. "This is for her. She was born with the wrong hands, too."

As Tabitha exited onto a Chinatown sidewalk, the petite knife shoved deep in her coat pocket, the doll in her purse oblivious to the encounter, she felt silly thinking herbs and spices could change her. She walked away from Chinatown as the meager December sun set behind a curve of buildings. Her husband was stuck at work, making spreadsheets and collecting numbers, which gave Tabitha a little extra time to haunt her favorite store.

On days when she felt especially out of sorts, the relationship between her and her hands strained to the point of wearing gloves even at home, Tabitha bought a doll from a store that sold dolls and antiques, an obligatory combination for wealthy city women who acquired both old dolls and the old furniture to set them on. Each new doll felt right to her at the time, almost as if their inaudible inner lives connected on some special frequency.

Today's doll shone beneath a track light off to the side of the store's main window display. The doll was not an angel or a showstopper, didn't wear a fancy dress or a seasonal halo. Her peach-colored lips bore no lipstick. But her hands! Perfect creamy seashells Tabitha cupped over her own much larger ears as she exited the store in a wet bluster. She never named her dolls or made up a convoluted doll history; they did not have books written about them; they were not born in a cabbage patch.

Tabitha tucked her new doll, half the height of a Barbie and with a topknot of brown embroidery floss, into her pocket along with the busted glove finger and the tiny baby knife.

"Cut off my hands and trade them with someone else? I should report that man to the Better Business Bureau," Tabitha said to her pocket. (She didn't forget to acknowledge her previous doll, who lay content in the bottom of her purse amid stale cookie crumbs. When a new doll came into the picture, though, the old doll knew to keep her distance.)

Happy hour approached. Tabitha loved the hopeful potential of a good happy hour. In the tiki bar around the corner from the antique shop, she requested a cozy table for two near the window.

"Will you be meeting someone else?" the hostess asked as Tabitha removed her coat.

"No, it's just us." She unwrapped her new doll from its tissue paper and placed her in a sitting position on the table next to a tiki candle. "I'll have a Mai-Tai and some Crab Rangoon." She scanned the retro cartoon menu. "And my new friend here will have a Queen Charlotte Fruit Punch." As she ordered for her, Tabitha pointed to her latest doll, who stared straight ahead. The server wrote down the order without looking up.

Under the glow of yellow tea lights, Tabitha ate her appetizer. Spicy ketchup wicked off her leather fingers. She left her gloves on, chagrined that her new doll did not come with gloves. "So be careful with your punch, okay?" she spoke toward the doll and her uncovered hands.

A table of twenty-somethings drinking Mai-Tais stared at Tabitha as they collectively sucked the rum from their lime garnishes. "Look at her," Tabitha heard one woman say. "And what's with her date?"

"Audrina, come on," said another voice in an indiscernible sea of highlights.

"Total psycho," someone answered.

"Maybe now, but you can tell she used to be pretty," the same kind voice replied.

"Don't you listen to them," Tabitha said. "Just enjoy your pineapple punch." She wiped spicy mustard off the doll's petite calico sleeve, leaving a little yellow dab, a blemish on her doll's left hand.

Things had changed since Tabitha moved to the city two decades ago to be closer to all the psychics. Back then, young women respected the misunderstood, sometimes even revered, eccentricities of older women. As she sucked the crab from her last deep-fried wonton, unconcerned whether fishy grease splattered her gloves when she pretended to feed her doll the tiny, most tender final morsel, she remembered the Grand Dame of the Bijou Café.

When Tabitha first moved to town, she ate every breakfast at the café, decorated to look like something from a very American version of Paris. The Grand Dame, who Tabitha could never stop watching, carried a stuffed dog each time she entered the Bijou. A man trailed behind her with a rhinestone-rimmed dog dish, which he filled with ice water and placed in front of the stuffed animal. As breakfast lengthened to brunch, the woman chewing dainty mouthfuls of bacon and eggs, her companion would refill the dog dish over and over from the bathroom faucet without any hint of embarrassment. Tabitha still recalled her jealousy. She had never been loved that way, not even by her dolls.

She stood up, positioned her doll in the crook of her folded arm, and walked over to the giggling group. "I think all of you need to learn to respect people who are different."

The young women took pictures of Tabitha and her doll with their phones. One of them said, "I'm gonna tweet this to *The Tonight Show* and hope someone reads my caption on air."

The woman in the center of the group—she struck Tabitha as a Sara—put her phone away without taking one picture. While the others Instagrammed, Tabitha stared at the woman's classic French manicure. Such recognition zipped along her nerves as she examined Sara's hands, Tabitha almost dropped her new doll on the floor.

"Excuse me, miss," she said as Sara got up to leave. "I...I think you may have my hands. Which means I, in fact, must have yours?"

The woman exited the tiki bar without saying goodbye to her friends. She never looked back at Tabitha and her tiny doll. Of course, Tabitha followed Sara into the streets, nighttime descending as lights reflected their yellows and blues in the puddles of rain.

"Sara!" Tabitha yelled toward the young woman's back as the doll jostled in her arm. "If you'll just stop for a minute, what I have to tell you might change the course of your entire life."

The woman turned to look at Tabitha before she hopped onto an approaching streetcar, a car Tabitha missed by the final closing of its door. The stranger with Tabitha's rightful hands disappeared in a metal can toward uncountable rows of apartments past the downtown business district.

Tabitha's stomach quaked with an unease she hadn't felt since the time, all those years ago, her first psychic told her about the mix-up with her palms. She sat on the bench next to the streetcar line to wait for the next car heading in that direction, though she knew, of course, that she would never find the woman who possessed her hands.

Tabitha sat on the bench for hours, letting streetcar after streetcar pass. She decided she didn't mind the smell of moist air so much, or the way her one finger felt so cold when a drop of rain burrowed into her exposed flesh. She removed the chewed-off glove finger from her pocket and flung the red leather into the nearest puddle, where it floated like a stitch. The pocketknife and doll she removed from her coat. Were her doll's fingers strong enough for the task? Would it hurt? Would there be blood?

It was more difficult than she thought, steadying the little knife in such a small, but perfect, hand.

The Unfortunate Act
of Falling

The Simmons boy disappeared on the afternoon CNN reported a break in the Natalie Holloway case. As the newscast flashed in the other room, Joan Reynolds, one of the mothers who lived on Congress Street, poked blueberries into the gummy dough of gluten-free muffins. The last box of gourmet, sort-of-do-it-yourself baking in the budget until her husband went back to work. In the last year, fresh berries had taken on the quality of caviar, his unemployment leaving just enough in their joint checking to choose which bills to pay, which to ignore.

"Since when is this World War II?" Harry asked. He watched Joan ration the fat berries, five per muffin, with none left over to pop in each other's mouths.

CNN featured the scuba diving couple that filmed "a young woman's corpse" on a recent trip to Aruba. *I don't like that he's wearing a gold chain,* Joan thought as she peered around the corner of the kitchen to watch the interview. She returned to counting blueberries on the first commercial.

Even though a reporter broke in over the story to let viewers know members of law enforcement did not believe the bones belonged to Natalie Holloway, Joan felt a chill as she imagined what would have happened if the long-missing girl turned up on another mother's doorstep. No longer a teenager, maybe no longer even blonde. Lost and relocated, but not really dead.

Joan had a funny thing about dead blondes. Marilyn Monroe, Anna Nicole Smith, Farah Fawcett, that woman in her classics book club who died crossing the street right after the boring part of *Anna Karenina*. Joan thought every death of a blonde must be the death of someone's American dream.

The phone rang as Joan settled the muffins in the oven. She set the kitchen timer while Harry answered.

"Joan. Joan, honey, turn on the local news," he yelled from the hall.

The neighborhood loved Hunter Simmons the way all mothers and fathers love most, if not all, six-year-olds. Children filled Congress Street with the sort of laughter that made you want to sip hot chocolate in the winter and run through sprinklers in the summer. Before the recession, there were organic peanut butter sandwiches and endless birthday parties and parks and rec soccer games. The parents rotated chauffeuring and cheerleading and protecting the children from UV rays and harmful free radicals. Before the recession, Joan knew the names of every child on Congress Street, and whether they preferred the whole grain bread of their sandwiches cut on the diagonal.

Money changes things. Having no money changes things more.

Since the recession, the mothers of Congress Street averted their eyes as they chose the cheapest bread at the grocery outlet, always enriched, always white. Out-of-work fathers began to understand the intricacies of playgrounds, which girl pushed another too hard on the swing, which boy never got the courage to go hands-free down the slide. They all knew Hunter Simmons as a sweet boy who talked of dinosaurs and monsters. He never whined about having to eat white bread. When he went missing, last seen making funny faces as the park merry-go-round twirled him into a welcome dizziness, the local news broke in over the possibility of Natalie Holloway's bones.

That March evening a breeze combed the brown lawns. Porch lights flicked on an hour before darkness swallowed the street. All the mothers and fathers gathered on the sidewalk near the Simmons' house to approach as a united front. Camera crews floodlit the front yard. Police handled traffic. Everyone agreed, and knew they agreed without saying so, that Mr. and Mrs. Simmons—Dan and Molly—looked smaller than normal, grief having withered them as they teetered on the edge of their porch.

A local reporter asked what Hunter was wearing when Dan Simmons lost him at the playground. A reporter from the next largest town asked how long Dan looked away. All the fathers and mothers of Congress Street, except Dan and Molly Simmons, knew Hunter was never coming back. The ones who go missing never come back.

Everyone wanted to bring the tormented couple dinner as an apology for knowing this. The mothers and fathers of Congress Street drove in a caravan to the closest grocery store. Organic and beautiful, none of them had visited Seasons Market since the remodel, two years back, when they all had jobs and Hunter Simmons was four years old and alive.

The market's automatic doors opened onto an artisanal bakery, French macarons lined up in bright colors. To the left, rows of sushi nestled against electric-green pats of wasabi. The fathers and mothers of Congress Street let their children run toward the candy aisle while they ogled lobster tails and kumquats, saffron, vanilla beans, balsamic vinegar aged a hundred years. For those few moments, they let go of the mayonnaise and white bread, the generic orange soda, the American cheese and common Red Delicious apple of the Grocery Outlet across town.

Harry demanded they pull themselves together as he rotated bottles of merlot in his palm.

"I refuse to bring the Simmonses a casserole," Joan said. "Tuna and noodles will never show how sorry we are that Hunter is dead."

No one took notice of such a brutal faux pas. But pretending the boy would be back by dinnertime to bask in his tow-headed happiness would take away from Joan's enjoyment of fondling the newest gluten-free brownie mix. The neighborhood tragedy gave her the only reason to, for these moments, pull out of her own misery, displace every sad thought, regret, bitterness with the idea of a missing child. This act of shared anguish gave her an excuse to indulge in little luxuries she could no longer afford.

Another mother splurged on a six-pack of cola sweetened with cane juice. The mothers and fathers of Congress Street told their children to pick out as many organic candy bars as their hands could hold while they made their way to the self-check with imported olives and the store's best Roquefort. And no one used a coupon.

Back at home, with her gluten-free brownies, Joan left another couple to worry about feeding Dan and Molly Simmons. To tell the truth, she didn't love or even like Hunter as much as she pretended. Because of him, Joey and Jacob hadn't slept through the night in months.

Hunter and his monsters. And how many nights had Harry suffered through this bedtime routine? "You should tape them shut, Dad. All the windows. Yeah, and put traps under the bed. The ones like for all the dead mouses."

On the first night after the first day Hunter went missing, the twins snored beneath their sheets without a nightlight. They knew without being told, the way kids know, that Hunter's monsters were now after him.

Every time Joan closed her eyes, she saw visions of Natalie Holloway, as the media was calling the tangled mass in the scuba video. Not a missing girl until someone official performed the right tests; just a coral reef curved in a fetal position, a face like the face of Mars. Almost not a face.

The next morning, Harry woke Joan before he woke the boys. "The police found Hunter at the bottom of the ravine. How will we tell the twins?" he whispered.

"No way." She sat up. "No way." Her hands covered her mouth. "Did he fall?"

"Yes, he did."

Harry sounded flat, the way a newscaster trains himself to sound, except for the time when John Kennedy Jr.'s plane crashed and one of the big reporters teared up on the evening news. Maybe it was because the newscaster recited a poem about Camelot, and also probably because everyone thought John John marrying that tall blonde erased the suspicion of his father murdering Marilyn Monroe.

Joan wondered if Natalie Holloway's blondness brought her more public tears than a brunette.

"I can't believe he just wandered away like that," she said. "I always thought he was such a clingy kid."

Harry said, "I won't tell you the way he looked when they found him. It'll put bad pictures in your head."

Who are you to be in charge of the pictures in my head, Joan thought. *Maybe we all need bad pictures in our heads to distinguish the good ones.* She burrowed under the covers and shut her eyes until Harry woke the boys and took them for a walk, in their pajamas, without breakfast first.

Under the covers, Joan realized she felt happy for the first time since the recession. The feeling crept up on her with an insidious certainty she knew not to question, a fabulous secret between Joan and herself. She felt rescued from the mire of her own thoughts as she sleepily imagined her once overfed body fattening back up, not from beluga caviar or Brie de Meaux, but from the joy of another person's sadness not being her own personal sadness. In fact, she already felt so bloated with joy, she managed to cancel out the thought of Harry wandering up and down Congress Street, avoiding the Simmons house as if he and the twins could catch their unhappiness and drag it home.

Joan got up and changed into a pink sweater. Almost the color of her skin, the sweater clung to her like a peel. She was wearing this pink sweater because she was alive and Hunter Simmons was not. Not that she was happy he was dead. Not exactly. She drove to the store without balancing her checkbook and bought two pints of blueberries for pancakes, the twins' favorite when she sprinkled cinnamon like intricate strands of DNA into the batter. On the drive home, she noticed other mothers and fathers of Congress Street sipping margaritas on their decks, stippled in late March shade. Boys and girls galloped in their pajamas. Some fathers allowed their children to trample the first crocus blossoms while others passed out cigars.

On the morning an ambulance drove away with Hunter's covered body, everyone except Dan and Molly Simmons felt like throwing a party. The fathers and mothers of Congress Street assigned tasks over back fences and across sidewalks. Balloons, canapés, a first-rate DJ. This was the boom, back and cranked on high.

Joan added organic soymilk to her pancake batter. The twins played Horse with Nerf balls in the front room while Harry stared at his wife whisking away the lumps. The more she stirred, the more they both remembered, without having to say a word, how the sight of pancake batter once signaled the slow-bubbling kickoff to a very ordinary weekend. During the recession, there were no weekends for the fathers and mothers of Congress Street to plan quick runs to the hardware store or indulge in a double-scoop cone downtown. Each day became a day to file with the unemployment department until the notice came that your days were up.

"They asked Lloyd to take a skills test," Harry said through a mouthful of pancake with too many blueberries to count.

Joey drank from the syrup bottle when Joan faced the stove to flip another short stack. With his fork, Jacob tilled a small pancake centered on his favorite plate. Joey moistened the indentations with syrup that disappeared into the folds.

"Must we talk about this during breakfast?" Joan asked.

"But a skills test means they don't think his job is coming back."

For a moment, Joan succumbed to the price of berries hovering behind her thoughts. It was too late to take them back, and she had already decided to refuse if Harry asked.

"How can they 'skills test' the former editor-in-chief of the newspaper? This entire town used to bend over backwards to kiss Lloyd's ass," he said. "I refuse to believe this mess came from importing everything from China."

Two hours past the announcement of Hunter Simmons' death, the happiness of the house began to dissipate. All over Congress Street, the mothers felt the fathers turn back in on themselves. The fathers watched the mothers turn down the thermostat and put on another sweater. Three hours after the death announcement, the phone began to ring. Patty Arthur from across the street withdrew her offer of canapés for the night's block party. Brad Holmes called Robert Bender to say count him out on renting folding chairs. There would be no helium tank to plump a thousand balloons, no DJ, no apple pie maker or barbecue steak flipper.

By late afternoon, the mothers and fathers of Congress Street had all sent flowers to Dan and Molly Simmons. By late evening, Joan had thrown her pink sweater into the hamper. The sweater, cropped and petite, still filled the entire wicker basket, which looked too small to hold a sleeping housecat. The day before Hunter died, Joan knew her hamper was deep enough to hold all of the twins' clothes, plus four of Harry's thickest argyles. She felt too tired to contemplate the hamper. She put on her pajamas. She scanned the Internet for coupons.

That night in bed, Harry tried to comfort Joan by untying his pajama bottoms. His erection became a symbol of wanting her in spite of dropped medical insurance and a canceled trip to St. Remy.

"But I can't talk about Provence while you have an erection."
Harry turned from Joan to tuck himself back into his
flannel folds. He slammed off the side table light, shocking
the room into darkness. "Since when does a couple go on
vacation and not think about sex?"

"Listen," Joan tried to reassure him, "I didn't mean to
sound so harsh. It's just that I got used to not worrying. I
know it hit quick. And I know I loved the feeling so much,
I convinced myself it could be our new reality. Not worrying about whether we can afford blueberries. I don't even
like blueberries all that much."

Their king-sized bed felt small enough to touch Harry without stretching. Joan grappled for the back of his
pajamas in the dark, wondering if this was how Natalie
Holloway felt before she died, like there was no point in
having fingers if they refused to hold on—to a handful of
sand, to the side of the boat, to the debilitating perma-
nence of water.

Harry turned back to Joan. "I know it sounds impossible, but I got used to it, too. And I know it makes me a
terrible person. It was only for one night."

"Plus three hours this morning."

When Joan considered unbuttoning her pajama top
so Harry could pretend to find novelty in breasts he had
touched thousands of times, she pictured Natalie Holloway's skeleton between them. She knew it was wrong to
resent Hunter Simmons' bones in a bag somewhere downtown, his death too small for CNN.

Harry curved his chest toward Joan and she settled her
head on his collarbone. "Did Hunter really just fall? He
wasn't abducted or, you know, worse?"

In the black safety of their bedroom, Harry's disembodied voice answered, "The poor bastard was just a stupid kid who probably chased a butterfly until he looked up and it was too late. But don't worry about the twins. I swear to you, I won't let them out of my sight until they are old enough."

"Old enough?"

"To know better."

And just how old is that, she thought. "Can you scoot over?"

"I'm on the edge," Harry answered. "In fact, my right leg is hanging all the way off."

Joan gripped her side of the bed with a foot to keep from sliding off, too. "Everything was so much better, and bigger, before. Look at us."

"And how is it possible we can't even fit into bed now? What happened to the room for an extra pillow between us?"

"I don't even want diamonds or dinner out. I just want to be able to not worry about blueberries anymore." Joan felt her eyes moisten. "And don't even get me started on *real* vanilla beans."

Before the recession, Joan sometimes spent close to fifty dollars a week on the beans, one pod per glass beaker. Some home chefs prefer chipotle, or smoked paprika, or whichever herbs-de-Provence Anthony Bourdain stamps with his cussing seal of approval. Joan loved vanilla even more than she loved blueberries. She found sensuality in the splitting of pods, the scented fuzz, the removal of all those tiny seeds. With the seeds she flavored cookies for the boys and crème brulee for Harry. Sometimes she made a sauce for lobster. Sometimes, before the recession, Joan would open a glass beaker in the middle of the kitchen while Harry crunched numbers in his office miles away. The vanilla aroma overpowered Joan when she raised the beaker to her nose. One sniff, on the rare occasion two, and she tossed the beaker, bean and all, into the trash.

Joan pulled away like she always did during their hard times. "Jesus. What kind of grown—sane—woman mourns this asinine shit?"

"You know how tough it was for me to give up my membership to the club, both socially and professionally, so why don't we just go easy on ourselves and allow a little mourning?"

Joan felt herself grow even colder between the legs. "You don't think it's a little insane to mourn vanilla beans and golf clubs instead of a sweet boy's death?"

"But he wasn't sweet."

"I know. And I know it makes me sound like a beast, but the truth is I'm not upset about what happened to Hunter. I'm depressed that we found out so soon. Hunter disappearing made me forget everything else."

"But look at our house, look at our neighborhood. What else do we possibly deserve?"

"None of us deserve anything. It either is or it isn't, all of this."

Harry spoke in the dark. "It's ridiculous to think this 2,500-square-foot house surrounded by other 2,500-square-foot houses on a postcard-perfect suburban street means rough times." He was using his accountant voice, the voice that once pounded through Joan like unrelenting, kind of sexy, absolute power. Now Harry just sounded like a blowhard. "And I also have it on perfect authority," he continued, "that no one has ever died from not visiting Provence."

Joan felt the sensation of shifting waters. She had to sit up before she drowned.

"Babe, where are you going? Okay, okay, it was an asshole thing to say. Just please come back to bed."

Joan remembered what happened to the Millers' bungalow on the next street over, then, and wondered what had broken down inside her since the recession to make her forget. What a random memory—how the mothers and fathers of Congress Street had instructed each other, without really saying anything, to look the other way when Rod and Nancy Miller filled a basket with canned food at the Grocery Outlet. The first family near Congress Street the bank foreclosed on. Even the memory of Nancy Miller's expert tapenade at last year's neighborhood block party failed to change anyone's impressions. Considering herself to be one of the more worldly women on Congress Street, with her English degree and a near supernatural ability to bake pitch-perfect scones, Joan had walked over to the Millers' house a week after they moved away without leaving a forwarding address. She had the urge to see, maybe even touch, real loss up close. She circled the block four times without being able to find their bungalow, even calling Patty Arthur to ask for directions. Patty Arthur and Boyd Matters, even Holly Perris, no one remembered Rod and Nancy.

Dan and Molly Simmons were becoming the next pariahs, and Joan wanted to see the audacity of their house glowing under the moonlight before they, too, ceased to exist.

No matter what happened with the economy, March would never be warm enough to go outside without slippers. Joan nearly longed to become a moonbeam, and if that wasn't exactly the right way to say it, she wanted to feel swept up, propelled forward by an unnamable force. But first she pulled on her slippers.

Harry slept, but Joan refused to creep through her own house like she had something to hide. She clomped as loudly as anyone can clomp in woolly slippers, down the stairs, out the door and onto their front walk. Joan followed the silhouettes of dimmed streetlamps toward the Simmons house. It made sense to find their kitchen light still on, the only illumination in the neighborhood, creating a perfect golden diorama, growing larger with each of Joan's slippered steps until she was close enough to hide behind the hedge under Dan and Molly Simmons' kitchen window.

"Hello, Joan," Allison Davis from two houses down whispered.

"You're the last mother here." Ann Roberts shifted so close to Joan that their silk pajamas sparked when the sleeves touched. "Look at the size of their kitchen. When did they add another island? Or is that two more?"

Joan asked in what her mother would call an *outside voice*, "What the hell's going on?"

"Be quiet. This is our destiny."

Joan's knees popped. She silently blamed trading in her Organic Essentials for generic vitamins. She wondered if Natalie Holloway's waterlogged bones still popped. Did any of the other mothers tucking their bodies behind the hedge ache when they crawled close to what looked like a play behind glass?

Dan and Molly sat on either side of a feast. From Joan's vantage point, the table seemed to go on forever. She counted fifty-four dishes before giving up, blaming her eyes for deceiving her as she focused on a dish blazing a deep yellow from a charitable heavy-hand of saffron.

"And look, there's a lobster and quinoa casserole!" Joan nearly yelled.

"How can you tell it's lobster from this far away?"

"People like us used to be able to sense lobster in our sleep. And do you see Dan oinking his way through my gluten-free cookies? What kind of father has an appetite at a time like this?"

"Why make the food if you don't really want them to eat it?" Ann asked.

But everyone knew the answer. It was all for show. Before the recession, Joan burned half her daily caloric intake for show, tried to digest the roughage of twenty-grain bread and signed up for hotter and hotter hot yoga classes, made sure everyone knew about her nightly plan to learn conversational Mandarin from Rosetta Stone.

She scanned the Simmons' cornucopia of entrees paired with appropriate wines and whispered, "But where are all the tears?"

"I can tell Molly is sad because she's eating the torte instead of lecturing Dan on how women are beautiful at every size, though her size is always the best."

"You're right. That bitch never eats torte. I even heard she sold her engagement ring on eBay last year to keep paying for Pilates."

"They're chewing without registering. It's an emotional thing."

"Like an Oprah thing?"

Joan tuned out the chatter to home in on Molly Simmons: her crystal vase on the table laced with fresh flowers, her clean counter, and her mouthful of chocolate torte, with melted Scharffen Berger ganache all the fathers and mothers of Congress Street stopped tempering last spring. Things had gotten that bad. In the clarity that comes from studying the enemy, Joan saw something that all the other mothers of Congress Street missed. A moment before Dan Simmons flicked off his kitchen lights for the night, Joan watched Molly Simmons center the last bite of chocolate torte on her tongue. Then she closed her eyes, and she smiled.

Adrenaline strobed Joan's nerves. She thought she could almost hear her own trembling bones as she bent and thrust her hands through the mulch beneath the window hedge. She unearthed a rock the size of her fist, but Joan knew living on Congress Street had weakened her too much to throw a punch. The smell of earth heaved up her nose as clods of dirt tumbled into her pajama sleeves. She aimed the rock in the direction of the Simmons' kitchen window, forty-paned and smudge-free.

A second before release, Patty Arthur grabbed Joan's arm. "What are you doing? Are you crazy?"

Joan heard the rock drop. "I don't know. I guess I just don't know."

It might have been the moonlight. It might have been her slippers on the cement walk, but Joan turned and sprinted with the ease of a child down the length of Congress Street. She reached her house out of breath, scampered up the stairs, and woke Harry with a violent shake.

"They're happy. I mean it," she bellowed into the gloomy bedroom. "They're happy that Hunter died, and I'm the only one who can see it."

"Oh, honey, there's no way they can be happy. I'm sure you're only misinterpreting whatever it is you think you saw."

"You don't understand." Joan popped the buttons off her pajama top in her haste to change back into the pink sweater. Now she could practically bend her entire body down into the wicker basket, where the sweater disappeared at the bottom. Nearly breathless, Joan detailed the torte, the ganache. "With at least twenty ounces of chocolate on the first two layers alone! I've never seen a dessert like that in my life. It was two, three feet high!"

"Doesn't that mean," Harry stuttered, eyes half open but still far away, "some family on Congress Street is doing better than the rest of us thought?"

"Yes. Dan and Molly Simmons. That's what I've been trying to tell you, and I've already figured out what we can do to keep up."

Harry fell back to sleep. The clock next to their bed ticked in a way that reminded Joan of the night before the first day of school—a night where no one slept and most of the teenage girls felt fat and certain that at least two other girls would show up wearing the same first-day outfit. Joan suspected Natalie Holloway of being one of those blondes who slept with ease, knowing her tastefully bleached hair would fall in just-right waves over the crest of a sky-blue sweater.

Joan knew she had missed the last train to sleep.

And she knew it made her a bad wife, but sometimes she wished Harry would stop breathing. Only sometimes and not forever, but on a night like this, even her husband's breath became a cacophony.

Before the recession, Joan used the kitchen to cure her occasional insomnia. Sleepless nights back then that never occurred over worry, but maybe because of a bad day in her menstrual cycle or a pulled muscle from hot yoga. Prac-

ticed in the art of gastronomy, which she took as reading
Julia Child from cover to cover twice, she fancied herself
an amateur chef who knew how to dress whole chickens
and coddle sauces until they promised to never embarrass
her by separating. To avoid gaining an ounce, she permit-
ted herself one drag through each delicate sauce with her
French tip before pouring her butter and egg concoctions
down the drain.

She had only been playing.

Now she got out of bed and walked downstairs to an
early morning kitchen with the insomnia of the desperate,
the worried, the misunderstood. Joan decided to arrange
her mise en place beneath the track light over the kitchen
island, forced to substitute Wesson oil for cold-pressed
olive, the Morton salt girl's wet umbrella spreading a
dampness where Himalayan mineral salt once settled like
an overpriced sunset. Dust from a set of seldom-used Le
Creuset cooking pots floured the island when she blew on
the colored enamel lids. No one saved extra unemployment money to slow cook a cassoulet. But Joan, surrounded
by temporarily unnecessary things, knew her recession was
about to end.

Dan and Molly Simmons paid their overdue babysitter tab
with Patty Arthur's out-of-season, yet still show-stopping,
bûche de Noel. The sitter understood in her vague teen
way to consider the debt paid and move on. She carried the
log-shaped cake to the park after March turned into April
and people slowly forgot to feel as sad about Hunter. In less
than an hour, a group of sixteen and seventeen-year-olds
devoured the chocolate cake. Joan, who spent her afternoons

spying around the park, paying special attention to inter-
actions that drifted too close to the edge of the ravine
surrounding the playground, watched dark crumbs blow
over the swing sets and disappear.

Since Hunter died, she had trained her eyes to notice
the smaller things. At his funeral, Molly wiped her eyes
with what looked like a Louis Vuitton pocket square, LV
prostrate across the hills of soggy French silk. Dan collected
chèvre and quinoa frittatas and foie gras terrines, and only
Joan could tell both grieving parents had no intention of
returning the serving dishes.

The mothers and fathers of Congress Street took turns
to honor what the neighborhood started calling "anniver-
saries." A truffle mac n' cheese to mark the first week after
the funeral. More truffles shaved over a casserole dish of
Chicken Cordon Bleu to commemorate the first month
since Hunter died.

The prized fungus infused its slightly disturbing,
sexually reminiscent oils in the warmer spring air when
a grumbling Mark Perris, Joan's closest neighbor on the
right, carried the newest offering past her front porch
as she sat outside drinking a glass of iced tea. Her body
tightened at the smell of something so exotic and so un-
attainable in the never-ending assault of toppling off her
upper-middle crust.

"I can't remember the last time I had even a bite of
something so lush," she said toward the sidewalk.

Mark Perris stopped walking, as if frozen in a better,
more abundant memory. Then he turned and stared at
Joan like he was undergoing some kind of diabolical test,
the decision to pass or fail beyond his control.

"My last taste of truffle was at a dinner party before a play opening four years ago," he answered, then looked away like someone caught.

"Didn't you even steal just one teeny shaving for yourself?" Joan felt like Scarlett O'Hara, trying in vain to bait the disinterested Ashley. She kept on baiting.

"Holly said it's wrong to indulge, with grief all around us. She knows better about this kind of thing."

Joan scanned Congress Street. The laughter of children in thinner spring jackets, with their chronic runny noses, gurgled from the park three blocks away. Sunshine dappled the sidewalk. A sparrow was singing, though there wasn't really anything to sing about. Yet.

"I don't feel grief around us at all," Joan said. "Did you use the best Gruyere you could find? I'm guessing the answer is yes."

Mark Perris blushed. Slowly, he detailed masterful cooking techniques that rivaled hers. "Breast" clunked out of his mouth, heavy as a German swear word, and Joan wished to turn this into their safe word, as if the two neighbors were entering a sadomasochistic role-play, each tempting the other.

Lucky enough to still be wearing her pink sweater, three hours on the dining room clock until Harry came back from the unemployment office, Joan swooshed down the porch toward Mark Perris like toned cotton candy.

The temporary co-conspirators, blood brother and sister sealing their pact with Serrano ham, dug into the stuffed chicken with their hands. They took turns, one steadying the casserole dish as the other popped chicken pieces into their mouth, or swirled their fingers in the glistening sauce, or peeled off the truffle shavings the way you could once steam the stamp off a letter to collect the canceled postage.

Joan waited for the last, most delicate truffle slice to dissolve on her tongue. "Come inside," she told Mark Perris.

They both knew this had nothing to do with sex.

The couple chatted with the palpable unease of foreign dignitaries not quite fluent in each other's language. Joan only got Mark Perris to agree to murder one of the neighborhood children—his choice, of course—after an hour of listening to him sob about how God would surely strike him down, but life wasn't really worth living without money; that he would do almost anything to afford a bottle of Merlot placed at eye-level in the wine section of the grocery store.

"Well, getting rid of another kid won't bring you any money, but it will bring everyone else enough of a distraction from their own problems to feel happy again. For a day or two at least. Then someone else will take his or her turn pushing another kid into the ravine, and it will be your turn to be happy. What do you say?"

"I, I don't know. That all sounds very extreme, and extremely crazy."

"Crazy is in the eye of the neighborhood," Joan said.

"I just feel so, well, beneath my own self, reaching for the four-dollar bottles of wine on the bottom shelf. And I shouldn't even spend the four bucks right now, so I drink the entire bottle before Holly gets home."

Joan swallowed in a deliberate way that looked vaguely sensual. "If you do as I say, you won't have to drink any wine at all and you'll feel serenely drunk. Trust me."

Mark struggled to stand. "Don't you feel the least bit guilty about what you're asking me to do?"

Joan thought about Mark's question for so long that, when she looked him in the eyes to answer, she saw a moment of relief almost ease the tension in his face, until she said, "No."

The next week, when police recovered Mark Perris's body at the bottom of the ravine, Joan wondered if Natalie Holloway could still be alive somewhere, like the way that handyman held the Mormon girl, another blonde, captive for months. That girl made it out fine and went back to not drinking coffee or swearing.

"You really need to stop talking about the Holloway girl. It's not healthy," Harry said to Joan as he reached for the phone. He then agreed, while Joan pretended not to listen on the hall extension, to be a pallbearer at Mark Perris's funeral. "I only said yes because I don't believe the accusations," he told her after hanging up.

That Mark Perris was a serial child killer who lured another boy past the town park and toward the edge of the ravine with promises of ice cream.

Harry said, "And besides, they didn't find ice cream near Hunter's body."

"Maybe it all melted by the time they got to him?"

"I watch enough of those investigation shows to know..."

"Which are too graphic for my taste, by the way."

"Well, I watch enough of them to know the police have the technology to find even one miniscule, seemingly insignificant drop of melted ice cream in a million ravines rolled into one. Hunter slipped and we all know it. What's all this talk about ice cream, anyway?"

"It's because everything is always about ice cream. I'm thinking about adding it to my pancake batter. Melted, of course. Call it an experiment in richness. Call everything since they found Mark Perris a tribute to spontaneous luxury."

Joan's blueberries plumped and exploded as the pancake batter heated up, but this celebration, for all her bravado, felt unsatisfying. She should have known Mark didn't have the constitution to murder a child. He was the only neighbor on Congress Street who actually bought those candy bars at school drives every fall. Holly Perris had already fled the state, taking with her the need for the mothers and fathers of Congress to bake mourning casseroles. Joan had such a good recipe for one topped with cheesy tater tots. Kitsch in that way that would impress the other neighbors, and also make them chuckle a little, a joke at Joan's expense. She agreed in her mind to be the butt of countless jokes to bring a little levity back to her community. It was the least she could do, really.

Connor Hayden's parents threatened to sue any accomplice who was complicit in trying to lure him into the park and into the ravine, even pointing fingers in the local paper at Mr. Hopper, who owned the ice cream parlor and who sold Connor's double-dip chocolate cherry cone to Mark Perris.

"Like that old man could have known what was going on," Harry said. "Since when is buying a kid a treat grounds for a witch hunt? I still don't believe Mark was up to something so diabolical, something so totally insane."

"I guess I've heard enough about ice cream for one day." Joan felt her eyes moisten from the disappointment of choosing the wrong accomplice. "And I don't think talking about Natalie is an obsession any more than your 'mild interest' in fantasy football."

Joan had started calling her just "Natalie" after Mark Perris committed suicide. Making sense of the pretty girl's disappearance came easier on a first-name basis. It was like the familial tendency of calling Oprah only Oprah, or Jesus only Jesus. This homespun informality made Joan feel almost Southern and without reproach as she wondered if Natalie suffered. Then she wondered if Mark Perris jumped into the ravine to save little Connor. What a selfish act, sacrificing the possible happiness of the entire neighborhood to save one scrawny, farsighted six-year-old.

"I knew Mark Perris was too weak to go through with it," Joan said as her four-burner stove shrank to two burners. "Now this is smaller, too?" she wondered. "Or were there always only two? Twins."

The twins chased each other around the living room with blued mouths. When Joey moved or Jacob turned, they became a comet trail of only one little boy moving too fast through the world, his double-exposed ghost image trailing behind.

I need to stop dressing them alike, Joan thought. *I need to start putting my things in order. I need to start counting burners and measuring bedspreads.*

"What exactly was Mark Perris supposed to go through with?" Harry said as he grabbed one of his children close to the neck.

"Christ, Harry, you're going to make him choke."

"The boys shouldn't run around with food in their mouths."

They aren't "the boys," Joan thought. One egg divided, they still had their own identities. They weren't always a mirror for the other to gauge the world through. Joey liked spaghetti, Jacob preferred chicken. Jacob complained of allergies and bogeymen. Joey never put away his toys before bed.

"Mark Perris promised he'd take Connor with him, all the way," she answered.

"Boys, go get changed," Harry yelled, even though one of them, he could never tell them apart from the first ultrasound to now, stood close enough to almost touch. Once the boy and his shadow, the shadow and his boy, left the room, he asked his wife, "Are you trying to sound crazy, or is this one of those hormonal things a man should be too sensitive to mention?"

"We had a pact. Over shaved truffles. He swore he'd be able to do it. We only picked Connor because he wears glasses. Call it Congress Street eugenics."

"I don't understand what the fuck you are talking about right now."

Joan stretched her arms toward Harry. He refused to meet her with any sense of understanding, or forgiveness. "Oh, honey, I came up with the best plan. A plan to make us all happy, each man and woman on Congress Street in their own specific way."

"Plan?" Harry's face looked so pale, it frightened Joan.

"Just calm down, dear, please. With each successful death, those not involved would feel so happy. Happy to have something else to think about for a change. Happy that tragedy did not befall them. Just, well, happy."

Harry leaned against the kitchen table where the family had eaten each meal since the recession. The dining table, with its extra oak leaf and room for several sterling silver trivets and candelabra centerpiece, sat silent in the next room.

Harry tugged the syrup-sticky placemats onto the ground. He looked like he struggled to keep himself from falling.

Joan said, "Don't look at me like that. Dan and Molly Simmons are the monsters, not me. Quit staring at me like I disgust you."

"If I am disgusted, it's only with myself because, right now, standing here leaning against this table that really isn't a table because it's not safe, not anymore, I realize that you don't disgust me. You scare me, maybe even terrify me a little, but that's all."

"Well, I guess that's something. At least you're sparing me the incessant questions."

Harry stood straighter. "Only because you don't know any of the answers."

That's where you are wrong, Joan thought.

The suicide spike on Congress Street made national news. Anderson Cooper furrowed his silver brows as he spoke of a fence going up around the ravine, paid for by the government, with the same flagrant intensity he used to chronicle other natural disasters. Rumor said he and his crew were in the rudimentary stages of filming at the ravine, packing his single-serving cans of freshwater tuna, his wrinkle-free blue button downs.

Each suicide created another orphan. Each orphan moved away from Congress Street to wash up like driftwood at an aunt's farm or a cousin's townhouse. More than a few of the orphans still wondered each night, as they tried not to dream, why all the adults in the neighborhood had taken them out for ice cream.

Patty Arthur jumped two weeks after Mark Perris. Both of Dakota Walden's parents turned to bones in the ravine that winter, after rescuers called off the search until the snow pack melted. Soon there were too many jumpers to track. Of course there were talks of a documentary. Oprah shed a few public, waterproof mascara tears. Mr. Hooper closed his ice cream parlor, boarded up the walls like he was in the middle of hurricane season. He had weathered the low-carb craze by installing a sugar-free frozen yogurt machine and a four-holed topping bar stocked with exotic nuts. What he couldn't weather were all the AP photos of children he knew by name crying at the edge of the ravine, hands covered in melted ice cream, a few of the braver ones able to peer down at the parade of broken bodies below.

Joan should've just carried out the plan herself, systematically choosing a child every few weeks. The most successful people, she was coming to realize, get everything done alone.

By the time foreclosures toppled most of the remaining houses on Congress Street, only two couples remained: Joan and Harry, and Dan and Molly Simmons.

"It's a real shame things can't be the way they used to be," Dan said while Molly cut a peanut butter and jelly sandwich into fourths. She centered each petite triangle onto a tea saucer to add the illusion of abundance. Dan carried the plates to the Simmons' dining table by stacking them down his arm.

"Yes, a damn shame," Harry answered. He had taken to ruminating, the way a war vet details his own personal sands of Iwo Jima at every VFW coffee and donut klatch.

"I don't remember the way things used to be," Molly Simmons said. She cut a carrot into four pieces and carried the orange strips, slightly withered, to the plates for garnish.

Joan added, "Maybe the way things used to be wasn't even as great as we remember."

This was their attempt to create unity. Weekly dinners at each other's houses, taking turns with the burden to produce some kind of offering, the unspoken agreement that no meal was too meager. Even the time, a few weeks ago, when all Harry could offer was one can of strawberry Crush, the couples sipped the flat pink drink like it was Veuve Clicquot, their elbows rubbing around the table where there was once enough room for twelve formal place settings.

"I think Oven Choice is a very fine white bread," Harry said as he chewed a corner off his triangle. "You could almost make a panini with this kind."

Molly Simmons licked a peanut butter and jelly edge off her tiny sandwich. "We sold our panini maker last month."

"Panini are so overrated," Joan answered through a small mouthful of food.

Joey and Jacob chased the Simmons' cat through the marble foyer. The cat, denied soft food for months, hissed at the twins with a mix of contempt and curiosity. Their outgrown pajamas revealed an inch of vulnerable belly.

The twins were relegated to cat chasing after an exhaustive search for Hunter Simmons' old room. Their shared, vicious child logic deduced the possibility of forgotten toys waiting for them, but when they sneaked down the hall toward where his room used to be, all they found, all Harry and Joan found, too, was a wall.

Was this the same thing as the way CNN wanted viewers to believe Natalie Holloway's bones became a fortress
waiting to be unearthed by the scuba couple on TV, by
whomever put them there in the first place, by Joan as she
teetered, closer and closer each night on her evening walk,
toward the ravine.

Joan sacrificed all of her food stamps at the March dinner to mark the one-year anniversary of Hunter's death,
bringing both dessert and coffee to follow up the peanut
butter sandwiches. Chocolate Dream Whip pie in a gra-
ham cracker crust, instant coffee, a Pall Mall to smoke
four ways. The couples had given up waxing philosophic
about the tenderness of farmer's market English cucum-
bers months ago for a sinew and blood acceptance of their
new, pared-down life.

Joan chewed her slice of Dream Whip into artificially
flavored mush, a full slice she did not have to share with
anyone at the table, while Dan and Harry traded tips about
ridding oneself of the embarrassment of shopping with
food stamps.

Molly said through front teeth sheeted in pudding,
"You sure went all out this time, Joan."

"Well, it's because of the anniversary."

"Oh, you two should've reminded me. Happy anniversary to a fabulous couple. We're honored you chose to
share your pie with us."

Joan stopped eating her Dream Whip. Her fork clunked
on the dessert plate. "It's not our anniversary. It's, well, it's
yours, right? Yours and Hunter's, I mean. Actually, just
Hunter's."

Dan interrupted with a full mouth. "I'm sure we don't know what you're talking about."

Molly asked, "How did you know Hunter was the name we always thought we'd choose for our child, boy or girl?"

Harry said, "You must've told us that, back in the day. Before..."

"Before it got too expensive to feed ourselves, let alone a child. I don't know how you do it, and so wonderfully, with two." Dan licked the final smear of Dream Whip off his plate without apology.

Joan thought of the near-religious fervor two people can create between them, its fever pitch built on a foundation of forgetting. Was this a couple's way to handle their grief, by shoving it down until it disappeared? Had Dan Simmons boarded up Hunter's room like it was never there, a tomb of plastic toys? Or, was Hunter never really there? A boy, a pink sweater, a bone—when these things disappeared, organic vegetables, did that mean they were never real?

Over the final dregs of instant coffee, Molly Simmons attempted to direct the strained conversation in a more positive direction. "I hear they are predicting an end to the recession."

Joan asked, "Who's they?" but no one answered her. She could no longer remember the color of Hunter's hair, his favorite game.

"And that'll mean an increase in the value of all things." Dan cleared the dessert plates.

Joan said, "True, but who will buy the houses of all those people who killed themselves?"

"I still think most of those were accidents," Dan said. "Unfortunate slipping. In fact, from now on let's all call it the unfortunate act of falling. Did you hear Bressler's 40

Flavors opened up downtown, where Mr. Hooper's place used to be? If an ice cream parlor can overcome the recession, so can the rest of us."

Joey and Jacob stopped torturing the cat at the words "ice cream." Even they knew, at nearly seven years old—the combined experience of fourteen years—how their parents sometimes talked in hushed voices and sometimes spoke in a way that didn't really fit what they were speaking about. Over the months, which seven-year-olds only understand by whether it is warm enough to play outside or cold enough for hot chocolate, their parents had discussed ice cream parlors in a tone that made them feel the way Hunter Simmons used to make them feel, when he talked about being scared of the things that hide in the dark. The twins knew that everyone's real terror was waiting for them when the lights come on.

"They had their grand opening yesterday, complete with balloons, candy red ones, and even a clown," Molly said. "We almost invited you guys, but weren't sure, you know, about whether you could, well, whether you could afford one cone for just one boy, or two."

"Well, since they started out as one egg, they can probably share," Joan said, feeling regret as soon as her mouth closed again.

She thought Molly almost looked genuinely sad for the first time since Hunter died. Hunter had existed. Joan was starting to think that she was the crazy one on Congress Street, but he was real. She remembered him, and more, she remembered the ecstasy his death gave her. She knew, after time had passed, that it was wrong to feel good about the death of a child. But she'd been so sad for so long.

Maybe Molly Simmons had also been sad all along—devastated, really—and that smile Joan saw sparkle at the edges of Molly's mouth while she stood outside her kitchen window a year ago, rock cocked and ready to crash through the panes, was only indigestion, or nerves, or a flash of a memory of Hunter doing something so specific only his own mother would understand the need to wish the memory away. The same way Natalie Holloway gradually faded from the news again, the death of any blonde the death of something more important than everyone's American dream.

"Why don't we throw coats on the boys and go now, before the ice cream parlor closes?" Joan said.

"But the boys just had pie," Harry answered.

"Look at them," Molly said. "They could burn off a triple scoop in about ten minutes."

"Come on, everyone. Let's just leave these dirty plates and go." Joan negotiated spring coats around the boys. They smelled of pajamas and sweat. They exhaled chocolate pudding as they raced down the walk.

Unwound

"It's not like being around a bunch of preteen girls turns me on or anything." Lara had grown tired of explaining herself to each new boyfriend when, in the course of their relationship, talk eventually turned from a mutual disdain of farm-raised salmon to the sharing of their sexual fantasies.

She preferred to keep her fantasies to herself. Wasn't that the point—letting one's mind wander without censure, no matter who, or what, turned up?

Her newest boyfriend, Thaddeus, tried to steer Lara from her summer camp story just like every other past boyfriend. "I don't want to get involved in some Chris Hanson *Dateline*-type thing, you know, where they set up a sting to catch guys who want to have sex with underage girls."

It's because men never listen the way women want them to listen, to each word that forms each sentence that, in turn, forms the push and pull of romantic unions. What

Lara wanted from Thaddeus was the same thing she had wanted from Paul before him and Rudy before that. Lara longed for someone to hear what wasn't being said.

She said, "I never once mentioned underage sex. That's horribly gross."

Thaddeus prematurely checked the Belgian waffle maker. The new couple's breakfast stuck, undercooked, to the top iron. "But you just told me whenever you touch yourself, you imagine summer camp when you were twelve?"

Lara sighed. She picked the burning waffle off the griddle with a fork. The dense sponge fell onto the counter in four small triangles. "I guess with a name like Thaddeus, I thought you'd understand. I thought you'd be, you know, different."

"You're right, you're right," her boyfriend of three months said. He stirred sour cream and powdered sugar to make waffle topping. "Try me again. I'll be open-minded this time, I swear."

Normally Lara would not try again. With the other men, whom she'd met by passing their age and weight preferences on online dating, Lara gave up after the fifth date. It was always around this time when her suitor showed up at her front door with a music box that played "Lara's Theme" from *Dr. Zhivago*, complete with a glowing, near-euphoric realization that Lara was *the* Lara from the story, a modern-day Julie Christie in the flesh, though Real Lara, with her unspectacular eyes and split ends, looked nothing like Movie Lara.

If I looked like Julie Christie, I wouldn't have to Internet date in the first place, she thought as she stacked each new music box next to the previous one.

Most of the music boxes, eight at last count, came from eBay. In what looked like a surreal installation piece in a twee gallery, the boxes sat next to one another, ready to play the tinny refrain, "Somewhere my love, there will be green and gold." Made in Japan in the early seventies, these boxes comprised a round plastic base of faux wood topped with a baby squirrel who sat on a swing set, swinging in time to the music as his squirrel mother kept watch from a porcelain tree.

Thaddeus had not given her a music box. He did not want her to be Julie Christie as Lara, but Real Lara. Lara who needed to trim her hair. Lara who worked part-time coordinating poets to read and sign books once a month at the public library. Lara who touched herself, late at night after the rest of the cul-de-sac went to bed, to thoughts of summer camp.

Not to thoughts of other girls in her bunk, the Chipmunks cabin of four girls waiting at the edge of puberty. That's where all the other men heard wrong. Lara did not pleasure herself to thoughts of vanilla cupcake-scented drugstore roll-on perfume, or even Marie-Marie, the girl so beautiful, so inviting, her parents named her twice.

It was the memory of the black ribbon that, without fail, always brought her body cascading into bliss.

Her summer camp cabin of Chipmunks joined forces the first week of camp with the Spotted Owls next door. Known among campers as the "advanced girls," the Owls, twelve going on twenty, already knew how to apply eyeliner. They spoke in a secret girl language that revolved around tampons and the Two Coreys and whether or not, when they got home, it was time to pack away the My Little Ponies and spend their extra allowance money on *Tiger*

Beat. The magazine had crowned Phyllis, the oldest Owl at twelve and a half, a finalist the month before in the "Color in Simon LeBon's Hair" contest.

"It's because I used nail polish instead of crayons," Phyllis bragged through a purple mouth stuffed with grape Hubba Bubba. "The paper still reeked when I tore it out and sent it in, even though I waited until the polish dried."

One of Phyllis's cousins, twice removed, took a job as junior camp counselor halfway through the summer season. This fact turned Phyllis from the lead Owl to the lead Everything. This meant she could now request after-hours ghost stories. Only other Owls and two of the Chipmunks—Lara and, of course, Marie-Marie—received invites through a complicated series of hand gestures, culminating in a to-the-death game of cat's cradle with two of Phyllis's favorite pink hair ribbons.

The night Phyllis's cousin showed up with her boyfriend, all acid-washed jean shorts and moussed hair, Lara knew something in her life was going to change. As a twelve-year-old, she assumed her life would change for the better, the direct opposite of what change now signified, forty years old and burning through every online dating profile in both her county and the next one over.

Phyllis's cousin's boyfriend, Rob, asked Phyllis's cousin, Cynthia, to stand near the small fire lit just for them after lights out for the other campers, the ones who wrote too many letters home and toasted each side of their marshmallows, prostrate on hand-whittled sticks, until a uniform beige blushed the entire warm and sticky treat. The Owls burnt every marshmallow until its cremains fell into the fire, too much gossip and too much laughter taking precedence over the simple task of rotating a stick in one hand.

They will all be bad mothers, Lara thought as, at the campfire with Rob and Cynthia, she fought against her obedient nature, her inner clock on alert that something, an object even as inconsequential as a marshmallow, needed tending.

From the shadows just past the campfire, Cynthia appeared in her regular camp uniform of T-shirt and knee-length shorts, but that night Lara felt a cosmic shift in her perception of the world.

Cynthia wore a black satin ribbon tied around her neck.

The image shook Lara, the ribbon giving the impression in the shadows that Cynthia's head and white blonde hair floated above her body. The other Owls gasped. Lara refused to fall for the optical illusion, but moved to stand closer to Phyllis and her charred marshmallow.

Rob then told the story of a teenage girl, just like Cynthia, who always wore a ribbon around her neck. Satin black. As Rob spoke, he pointed to Cynthia's neck. She curtsied, and Lara remembered how much Cynthia looked like a member of a royal court. In the story, the girl met the boy of her dreams. On their wedding night, which Lara couldn't really comprehend the gravity of since she had never even kissed a boy, the new husband asked his bride to remove her ribbon.

"But I can never remove this ribbon," Cynthia answered when Rob paused.

"Whyever not, my love?" Rob asked.

Lara loved how he talked so old-fashioned.

"Because if I remove the ribbon, my head will fall off."

Rob said the boy in the story became obsessed with slipping the ribbon off his wife's soft neck, so much so that at night he practiced slipping a ribbon, identical in both color and width, off one of the boxes of instant oatmeal they kept in the pantry while his wife slept.

This revelation caused a collective resonance to fan out among the campers with whispered observations like, "They wake up every morning and have breakfast together. You know what that means."

"No!" "Yes!" "No!"

"It means every night they fall asleep together. And if her husband is so concerned with removing the ribbon, that means he's already removed everything else!"

"Like when she sleeps, even her, you know, butt is showing?"

"No!"

"And they eat the same oatmeal my mom eats."

"That means your mom probably sleeps with her butt showing."

"No!" "Yes!" "No!"

For extra effect, Rob produced the same type of ribbon Cynthia wore. He tied the ribbon to Phyllis, who Lara saw blush, even in the flickering fire, before quickly untying the ribbon again. Then, as he moved to untie Cynthia's ribbon, she fell away from the fire. When he centered a flashlight beam to illuminate her face, a carefully placed camp-issued jacket gave the impression for a moment, deafened by delighted screams, that Cynthia's head had, swear to God and the other Owls and Marie-Marie, fallen off!

Lara asked Thaddeus to follow her thread to its final conclusion as he broke the crystallized sugar around the maple syrup cap. He filled each indentation in his second waffle to the brim. She picked at her waffle, cold from her absentminded mistake of too much sour cream topping.

She also noticed a small jar of jam Thaddeus had warmed on the stove.

Lara said, "I have never been the same since that night. Not because of my record-breaking crush on Rob or wishing I had white-blonde hair, but because I realized the length a man will go to, even risking the death of his beloved, just to reveal her one secret, whatever that secret is. Almost like I realized that night how the world is pushed forward by everyone's secrets."

"That's what you got out of that?" Thaddeus tucked a ripe blueberry into each syrupy pool. His waffle looked more like geometry than breakfast.

"I did. So the idea that someday, somewhere, I will meet a man who will risk my life just so he can see me fully exposed is my go-to fantasy."

The warmed jam looked like blood when Thaddeus dipped his thumb in the berry compote and rubbed a dark red line around Lara's neck. He looked into her eyes without glancing away. "This is how I mark you."

Lara felt her body slope toward him. If Thaddeus was not her ideal match, he was closer to fulfilling her fantasy than any man before him. As he slowly licked the jam line off her neck, even around the back of her neck without pausing when his tongue bumped against the resistance of Lara's hairline, she promised to do everything to keep him wanting to know all of her secrets.

The next morning, Lara greeted Thaddeus at breakfast— this time oatmeal, steel-cut from the fancy can—with a pink ribbon the color of a dyed Easter egg tied tight around her neck.

"Cute, but I don't know if the Victorian look suits you." Thaddeus sat at the breakfast table. He sprinkled brown sugar on his oatmeal, though Lara had already told him sugar negated the heart-healthy platform. "I know," he answered before she spoke, "but what can I say. I guess I'm craving something sweet after last night."

Lara stared at Thaddeus and his adulterated oatmeal.

"And I'm guessing, from the prim ribbon, that either you're really trying to land the school marm look or you, too, want more?" Thaddeus moved to untie Lara.

She pushed his hands away from her neck. "No, please don't."

"Oh, really?" Thaddeus shoved his oatmeal aside. "And why is that?"

Lara said in a very clear voice, "Because if you remove my ribbon, my head will fall off."

"Very funny." He placed his fingers close to the knot Lara had tied behind her neck.

She turned her body away just enough for it not to seem like overt rejection. "I mean it. If you don't drop your hands, I'll scream."

"Okay, okay. Whatever game this is, I guess I don't mind playing a little bit longer." Thaddeus picked at his sugary oatmeal.

With her pink bow constricting the momentum of her chewing, Lara finished two soft-boiled eggs. Lara guessed a woman whose head fell off if anyone removed her ribbon would never have breakfast in a kitchen that smelled of soft-boiled eggs.

"Wait, is this some kind of role-playing thing?" Thaddeus asked after he finished his breakfast. "Like *Fifty Shades* of whatever?"

Her breakfast plate still smelled of soft-boiled eggs. Lara stood from the table and cleared the dishes. "This," she turned from the sink and pointed to her pink ribbon, "just is."

In the following days, Lara wore a lemon-yellow ribbon, then a tan ribbon with laced edges. A blue ribbon the color of the famous Tiffany box followed the red ribbon Lara thought Thaddeus stared at more than any of her other ribbons combined.

A few weeks after the appearance of the first pink ribbon, he had asked her before bed, "So, if your head can supposedly fall off without a ribbon, how do you keep changing colors every day?"

"Do you want to see?" she asked.

"Right before bed like this?"

"Yes, it's the best time."

The black satin ribbon, an identical match in width and sheen to the ribbon Phyllis's cousin wore all those years ago at summer camp, Lara had saved until Thaddeus asked how she changed colors without eminent decapitation.

Of course she knew it was all just a game. She danced on the precipice of really liking a man, this man, so close to the edge, she worried about her boyfriend experiencing the first pang of boredom that unravels every knot of possibility. He would start to look at porn instead of at her. She would try to figure out what porn he looked at before realizing a woman with average-sized thighs could never compete. He would stay late at work. She would stay later at work to avoid finding out just how late he stayed.

Lara wanted to be with Thaddeus because he did rare, sensitive things, like buy her Sugar in the Raw to use in her coffee when she spent the night at his house, without her having to ask. He never called Lara a hypocrite when she poured four packets into each coffee cup while playfully castigating Thaddeus for his brown-sugared oatmeal.

As Lara smoothed the imaginary wrinkles from the black satin ribbon between her hands, she wondered what happened to Phyllis's cousin. Did Cynthia ever wear a black ribbon around her neck again? No doubt she had babies, maybe even grown-up children with their own babies by now. Lara knew to never tie a ribbon around a baby's neck. At least, she thought she knew. She wondered, if she had a baby girl, would her baby inherit her curse? Then she remembered this was all make-believe.

Lara had worn ribbons every day for weeks, so long the line between real and imagined blurred, like any couple's collective memory. Even if Thaddeus tore the ribbon from her neck, her head would stay securely attached; blood, bone, sinew, skin. She knew this the way she knew what she looked like before any obsessive examination in her bathroom mirror. Still, when she showed Thaddeus how she tied each new ribbon over the old before gently pulling the old ribbon out from under the new in a maneuver she had mastered like a sleight-of-hand magician, she felt a little scared. And maybe even a little bit heartbroken.

"But what do you do with the old ribbons?" Thaddeus asked. He stared at the striking black line.

"I fold them up and put them in a drawer in case I want to wear one of them again." Lara led him to her bedroom dresser to show off her ribbons.

"I find you so unusual," he said.

"Good," she answered.

The couple agreed not to get bored of each other, not to take each other for granted, not to do all those small things that ruin the big picture. Thaddeus stayed the night enough nights to only go home for mail and underwear. Then he stopped going to his apartment at all.

"Look, your first piece of mail with your new address. But I think it should be required by law that, once a man is engaged, the post office stamps 'Hubby-to-Be' on each piece."

"Even junk mail?" Thaddeus hammered in a nail to hang his framed college diploma in the home office they now shared.

"Of course." Lara wore a calico ribbon decorated in rhinestones.

"I would never do such a thing," Thaddeus said. He kept hammering.

Lara tugged at her ribbon. Was he getting tired of her charade to exist as a woman much more mysterious, at least one who held a deep body mystery involving decapitation by silk, than she actually was? In real life, the Real Lara liked to eat tuna noodle casserole. In real life, sometimes grey lint collected in her navel. In real life, her body, at least since her last doctor's visit, was hooked up the way every other body hooked up.

Thaddeus continued. "I could never do such a thing because I couldn't stand making the mailman so jealous he'd want to die, Wifey-to-Be."

Hubby and Wifey, sweet to each other in that sickening way people in public turn their heads to avoid. But Lara and Thaddeus existed in private, her house now their house, his manicotti recipe now her recipe, as ribbons wound like colorful snakes around every free space in every dresser drawer.

———

The evening before their wedding, Thaddeus cleared his throat at the dining table. He pushed away his half-eaten salmon filet. In a mock proclamation he announced, "It's official. I have decided I like the black ribbon best."

Lara wore the black ribbon. She caressed its sateen border. "I knew it. For all these months, actually. But I hope you understand I already committed to wearing a blue one tomorrow, as in Something Old, Something New. But, still, I knew it."

Thaddeus leaned in closer. He examined the thick black gash around her neck. "How did you know?"

"The way you look at me each time I wear it. The way you size me up, so to speak. The way I can tell you want nothing more than to take my black ribbon off."

Lara cleared the dinner dishes, careful to place the salmon skin and bones in a freezer bag before their disposal, the way the couple did every other task with care to never leave too much of a mess behind. They had even decided as a couple to spend the night before their wedding together. After sleeping in the same bed every night for over six months, they didn't know what else to do.

Thaddeus and his bride-to-be got ready for bed in separate bathrooms down the hall from each other, an early agreement that he would claim the guest bath as his own. No one needed to watch each other brush their teeth. Lara didn't want Thaddeus to discover that, even on the nights they showered separately, she kept her ribbon on. At this point she had repeated the phrase to her groom-to-be so many times, she herself was not positive her ribbon did not, in fact, hold her head in place.

Lara crawled into bed. Thaddeus asked, "How do you know I want to rip your black ribbon off your creamy neck while you sleep?"

The couple faced each other. City light from behind the bedroom curtain helped them see almost as clear as at daybreak.

"Because that's what you've always wanted to do." Lara brushed a sensual finger across her black ribbon. "Isn't that even why you proposed to me? Because you hoped beyond hope than on our wedding night I would remove my ribbon, and it would feel so close to having sex with a virgin that you would feel your own rebirth, in a way?" She stroked Thaddeus's handsome cheeks in the artificial blue light. "Both of us together, naked and innocent, the way no one's been allowed to exist since, well, since Internet porn." Lara giggled close to his ear as she molded her body into his.

"As naked as John and Yoko?"

"If not just like them, then very, very close." Lara turned from him to settle her body into sleep. "Except that I can't remove my ribbon, no matter how much I want to. Not even tomorrow night, and not even for you."

"What?" Thaddeus sat up in bed like his whole body felt an electric shock.

"It's simple, my sweet, delectable Hubby-to-Be. If I remove my ribbon, my head will fall off."

"But, you're not really going to wear a ribbon tomorrow, right? My grandparents will be there, and my mom already thinks we're moving too fast."

"And?"

"And I was hoping you'd try to, you know, be a little more normal. Just until we leave for our honeymoon."

Thaddeus's words disintegrated the collusion the couple had gotten so used to sharing.

Lara tied her black ribbon almost too tight to speak. "Well, I hate to break it to you, but I'm wearing the blue ribbon tomorrow. If I don't, my head will fall off."

Thaddeus jumped from the bed and flipped on the light. "What the fuck are you talking about? Are you fucking crazy? Is this all some sort of elaborate fucking joke to you?"

"Calm down." Lara felt to make sure her ribbon stayed secure against her neck. She gasped, then said, "And you know I hate it when you say the F-word."

Thaddeus stomped from the light switch to Lara's side of the bed. "Take it off!" he yelled close to her face.

"No, I told you. I can't."

He punched the extra pillow beside Lara. He yelled, "Do it! Now!"

Thaddeus stared at Lara like he wanted to strangle her with her own ribbon, his tender arms a flexing series of aggression. She could smell his warm body, the oily leftover salmon that would not rinse off his hands after dinner. His pupils narrowed to pinpricks of black in the celestial blue of his eyes. She had never guessed a baby-faced man with blue eyes the color of an antique glass bottle could make all the hairs on her body stand up from her skin.

"I told you I can't." Lara pressed the ribbon so tight to her neck she almost blacked out.

In an angry silence punctuated by the brusque movement of muscle becoming threat, Thaddeus snatched the ribbon from Lara's neck. The black satin gave to the strength of his fingers with one quick, ardent tug. He gripped the black ribbon, which seemed almost to squirm in his hand, like a hard-won trophy. He even thrust the spent ribbon toward the glaring overhead bedroom light before being released from his trance by his Wifey-to-Be holding her hands to her neck as she struggled to breathe.

"Oh, cut it out," he said. "We both know you're fine. Move your hair so I can see."

Lara slowly parted her long hair. Her neck looked just like Thaddeus had remembered, pale and unspectacular, without even a discolored line where Lara's ribbon had been.

"See, you're fine. Just like I said."

"Yes, I'm fine," she answered.

"We'd both talked about this so many times, in the back corner of my craziest thoughts, I wondered if what you said could be true, though I knew it was all just pretend."

"Yes, just pretend," Lara said. She stared at the pillow with the indent of Thaddeus's fist.

"I guess we should get some sleep before the big day, Wifey-to-Be." Thaddeus dropped the black ribbon onto his side table. In slick silence, it slithered to the floor. He turned off the bedroom light and edged slowly back into bed.

Lara spoke into the dark. "If part of you almost believed my head would fall off, why did you still remove my ribbon?"

Thaddeus rolled over. Lara turned from him. Neither wished the other sweet dreams.

The Compromise

Claire wanted to rent an RV. The one in the ad with the pullout bed, the efficient cupboards where every cup and plate knew its place.

Jack wanted to drive their car on vacation.

Claire wanted to stop at their favorite seafood restaurant with the view of the southern coast sea lions sunning themselves all afternoon.

Jack wanted to try the new place, already famous for a cut of steak that resembled a catcher's mitt cupping an entire grilled onion.

Compromise. This was how Jack and Claire ended up on vacation, driving their car but parking in the last spot of the steakhouse lot. His mouth prepared for meat. Her mouth prepared to order an overpriced salad for an entrée, one that didn't even come with bread.

"Nothing really comes with bread anymore," Claire said. The couple sat at a side table with a view of the coastal inlet. Claire rubbed the sweat off her glass of ice water. She placed her fingers against her cheek.

Jack wrote in the little red notebook he took on trips: "Discuss restaurant markups with C. when we get home. There will never be a salad worth $27. Is she testing me?" He closed the book and placed it back in his pocket.

Even after the salad arrived, without bread, Claire never asked Jack what he wrote. She did ask, "Do you like the way it's cooked?"

Jack cut the steak into bite-sized pieces. Each piece released a torrent of red juice across his plate.

"I don't think you're supposed to cut the whole thing right away," she said. "Doesn't that make it lose its moisture?"

"Sometimes a man just wants to eat a good piece of meat. Not everything has to have a deeper meaning, you know."

With her fork, Claire deconstructed her Cobb salad into separate mounds of chicken and avocado and slices of boiled egg. She focused on the greens beneath what she called the good, fattening stuff. "That's why I asked. Is this one of those times?"

"Well, I'm eating, aren't I?" he said.

She wished being thin didn't always mean ordering the salad. Visions of beef tournedos wrapped in bacon filled her thoughts. "I meant, is this one of those times when it is good?"

"Of course it is. We're on vacation."

The word vacation meant two different things to them. To Jack, vacation meant going south. At forty-two, with a career as a city planner and the economy on a slow up-swing, Jack felt certain, in the way only a middle-aged man who lost his hair ten years before can feel, that nothing good ever happens if one travels north. Urban sprawl, more snow, Canada teetering above with its confusing money and its fries smothered in gravy.

Claire loved to ski. She fantasized about learning how to make her own marshmallows after hitting the slopes. Big, fat squares Martha Stewart floated in an ideal cup of cocoa. But this was Jack's summer to direct them toward the southern Oregon coast. Cranberry bogs. Botanical gardens. Guidebooks dubbed the region not only the gateway to the redwoods, but also the "banana belt." While Jack used the restroom midway through dinner, Claire searched her phone for an exotic banana or cranberry recipe.

When he returned, Jack swallowed his last ring of grilled, blood-tinged onion. "Listen, hon, I know you wanted to go to the mountains this year, but it's been a hard few months, what with that last project not getting final approval, and I thought we needed to do something more relaxing."

"Okay," Claire said. She picked cranberries from between her molars while Jack asked for the bill. She maneuvered a wooden pick up and around each tooth. "These things have invaded my entire smile."

Would this incident become another poem? Back in their college coffeehouse days, Jack loved to listen when Claire read her poems at Friday night open mics. Who wouldn't want to be the lover of the woman who stood on a tiny stage reciting lines of verse in that irresistible singsong voice? Inevitably, Claire's poems began to star either the flesh and blood representation of Jack the Boyfriend, down to the reportage of his body functions and foibles, or Jack the Everything, idealized, a masculine specimen with the precise percentage of body fat to traipse through Claire's dreamier poems on a white steed, without one gallop of irony.

At twenty, all it took for Jack to feel heroic in his bones was the price of a house coffee and one of Claire's poems read so gently, she never got one fleck of red lipstick on her front teeth. Now Claire edited an occasional textbook of collected essays on poetic form. She still wrote poems. Not every day, but more than just "on the side," that term she hated. In Claire's recent work, what for the past decade she referred to as her "married poems," Jack was always HE. HE became the incentive to explore HER response to the myth of the dissatisfied wife.

Claire asked, "How come there are Craisins on everything in this goddamn restaurant, anyway?"

"It's the cranberry capital of the southern coast, or some shit."

"Why don't we go to that candy store across the street, then? See how the sign on the window says Free Samples. Don't you find that concept quaint?"

Jack heard the beginnings of another poem forming in Claire's head. She would craft a villanelle, her favorite verse form, with its five tercets and that zinger of a quatrain, about how everyone craves getting something for free.

"You're one to judge. You probably have the beginning stages of dysentery," he tried to joke.

"How did I ever end up marrying a man who not only hates women who order salad at dinner, but is an anti-Semite to boot?"

Jack figured out the tip while Claire juggled her small leather vacation bag until her sunglasses fit next to her wallet again. "I mean it, Claire. It just isn't a good idea to eat food from someone you don't know, especially on vacation. I don't care whether or not she believes in Jesus."

"But she was wearing such cute shoes. And you know I don't normally compliment women's shoes, but she was wearing the specific kind of shoes I would actually wear."

Jack paced the short expanse around their restaurant table. Knowing the next vacationing couple in a long line of wives ordering salad and husbands gorging on steak waited by the host station made Claire's words resonate even less than usual.

"Her shoes made us sisters for that moment in the used bookstore. My unquestioning love for her shoes is why I bought that copy of *Catcher in the Rye*."

"Which we already own four of." Jack signed his name on the credit card slip after leaving what he viewed as a respectable tip.

"But she used to be a professional baker before she bought the bookstore. That's why she brings in homemade rugelach. And she never makes it with store-bought pie-crust, like all the other cheats. In fact, Sarah..."

Jack stared at his wife's tilted forehead while Claire wiped her side of the table free of crumbs. "You know her name?"

"Of course I know her name." She left three more dollars in the guest check holder. "And like me, she loves *Seymour* way more than either *Raise High the Roofbeams* or *The Stories*. Well, except for 'Bananafish,' but that's obvious."

One person in the couple always walked ahead of the other, or fell behind. "I don't understand how you recover from being so intimate with someone you'll never see again," Jack said to Claire's back.

They walked toward the store famous for its cranberry candy. Claire crossed the street before the light gave her permission. "Relationships can be just as meaningful whether they last five minutes or five decades," she said without looking at him. "That's the way I've decided to look at things, and so far it's worked."

Jack and Claire grazed through the rows of free samples, dissolving on their tongues everything from cranberry-flavored Turkish delight to cranberry fudge. They smiled at the ardent tartness of cranberry taffy, great bins of hot pink candy with darker jewel centers. Both expressed neutral feelings for the cranberry tea cookies. With a deep bodily rejection of the store's proprietary cheddar cheese fudge, Jack and Claire walked closer together as they exited the store. He held out his hand at the crosswalk. She accepted.

To their families, they were either Claire and Jack or Jack and Claire, one name piggybacked on the other for so long that when someone addressed Claire as an autonomous being, or Jack as a man unto himself, something fell flat to the couple's ears, though Jack had always suspected he enjoyed belonging to a couple more than Claire enjoyed sharing a last name and a credit score. In the middle of the street, she dropped her husband's hand. Claire made it to the other side first.

"It's too early to check into our hotel," Jack said, winded from indulging in too many cranberry-infused sweets combined with running after his wife.

"We could paint pottery?" Claire pointed to a corner store, opened since last year's annual attempt to create memories in someplace other than their shared hometown.

"Remember that old saying about real men not eating quiche? As far as I'm concerned, they don't paint pottery, either. Why don't we rent beach cruisers and putter around for an hour or two?"

"I know you don't accept salad as a real meal," Claire turned from the pottery lounge and the sound of couples deciding which piece of unfired bisque to christen as their vacation keepsake, "but I am too stuffed to bike anywhere."

"Why don't we compromise with a drive instead?"

Claire knew that in her role as wife of Jack, the man who worked long hours so she could stay home, she was called on to pretend going for a drive equated a compromise. A scarred fallopian tube meant she did not stay home to raise children, though she knew by fifth grade, watching the grainy school health film, that she did not find the story of how a female body becomes pregnant the least bit intriguing. Claire spent most of her days writing poems. Some years this produced a few thousand dollars earned in contests or a *New Yorker* piece. Other years, while Jack worked to revitalize the fringe neighborhoods that edged their city without seeming like the city was anti any ethnicity, Claire wrote nothing for months at a time. She luxuriated in not having to leave the house if she didn't feel like facing an eyelash curler or the congested artery of traffic that funneled her neighbors toward the shopping district. Other afternoons she treated herself to plates of palak paneer or a salt-and-pepper pedicure or a giant cappuccino before walking the length of the downtown area with a caffeinated buzz. Last fall she'd taught herself how to make buttercream frosting. Before that, how to distress furniture with a hammer and an ice pick. Because Jack's job meant designating vacant lots to be turned into mixed-

use areas dotted in parks, Claire could cry while reading
Sharon Olds in the middle of a Tuesday afternoon under
the shade of an aspen in Jack's newest park without having
to feel embarrassed. This also meant, on vacation, they did
not paint pottery.

"Yes," she said, "a drive sounds nice."

"How about we check out that national park up the
road? I've heard raves about the redwood trees being so big
a photo doesn't do them justice."

How unlike Jack to suggest such a spontaneous plan.
Her Jack, with a body she once fantasized about so often,
her hand cramped. Her Jack, with a body now too tired to
let her undress it, too tired to yield to the pleasure she still
offered up as easy as breathing, coupled with a mind too
obsessed with gentrifying the nearest town over to relax in
the elocution of her tongue pronouncing each of his most
private parts with a slow, categorical lapping.

Jack and Claire drove toward the national park, a few
miles past their motel. He said, "I've always thought it's
ridiculous travelers can't check into their rooms until after
four. Why can't we just check in at eleven, or noon?"

A combination of cranberries and cheddar fudge coated
Claire's throat each time she swallowed. She felt too lazy
to ask her husband to stop at the gas station so she could
buy a Coke. "When would the rooms get clean that way?"

"I personally don't see how all the Rosaritas and the
Magdalenas signing their names on those sad tip envelopes
really do much difference. I doubt they even change the
sheets, unless there's an obvious need."

"Oh my God. Now you really do sound racist."

Claire regretted not asking her husband to stop for a
Coke. The first time she saw one, she would insist on

asking Jack to pull up in front of a Mexican bakery, only she would call it a *panaderia*, to buy the coldest bottle of sugary-sweet Mexican Coke in the place, and not offer him a single sip.

"Please. When's the last time you saw a hotel maid that was either white or didn't move like a bloated brown slug?"

"Jack, I don't understand what's gotten into you. Is this because of the bodega debate? Is what they keep reporting on the news really true?"

The couple stopped their car behind a long row of other vacationers waiting to get into the park.

"You know what, I'm getting really sick of our community turning their vitriol on me. I only asked the planning commission to move a few of their stores away from the new downtown park. You know they sell the same things at each one, row after row of those shitty pink cookies and Jesus candles and tacky *piñatas*."

"What would you say if I told you I want you to move out when we get home?" Claire placed her salt-and-pepper pedicured feet in front of her on the dash, mostly because Jack hated when she sat that way.

"I'd probably say I don't believe you."

She spoke calmly. "What if there's a part of me, a part that is slowly coming to the surface, that likes being alone more than she likes being married to you?"

"Then who will pay for those?" Jack pointed to Claire's white toenails tipped in black glitter.

"I guess I'll just have to learn to go without." She stared out the open car window. She did not notice how redwoods crowded every side of the national park's main entrance.

"But how will you live without your expensive Indian lunches? And who will buy all those biographies of Emily

Dickenson for you?" Jack honked at the traffic standstill. He yelled toward the windshield, "Why won't this goddamn trailer move up?" before he said to Claire, "I know one thing I won't miss when I move out are those godawful bricks you try to pawn off as Emily's fruitcakes each Christmas." Jack stretched his head out of his car window. "Hey, asshole, move it!"

"First of all, over ten percent of Emily Dickenson's poems mention food or drink at least once..."

"I know, I know."

"And second, I can't believe I'm choosing to agree with you, but that guy should move up so we can get the back of our car off the road."

"He's not moving because he's another entitled dickhead in a very long line. Haven't you heard that on vacation, the lines stretches to infinity?"

Claire dropped her feet from the dash. She shuffled back into her espadrilles, as if at any moment the universe was going to call her to action. Staring at the side of Jack's face as he continued to curse the RV, she asked, "Why don't we teach them a lesson?"

"Like not to mess with a couple like us?"

Then Jack laughed. Claire's heart beat faster each time her husband laughed. She almost thought he had forgotten how.

Jack stopped honking. He turned to look at her. In between more giggling he said, "We could follow them to their campsite and really make them sorry."

"It's a deal." Claire shook her husband's hand.

"Seriously, I wish all the rude, obnoxious people of the world could be put in their place, one RV crammed full of portable DVD players and s'mores kits at a time."

"Jack?"

The RV in front of them honked for the couple to back up so they could turn around.

"Jesus!" he yelled. "Now this prick's acting like we're in the wrong. Hold on, asshole!" The driver of the RV, when the couple got a better view, looked the same as Jack. A man on vacation with a wife who resembled Claire.

"Maybe they just want to get out of here?" Claire said as Jack backed up. "They didn't even get to see the trees. And I bet, if she's like me, she regrets bringing ballet flats on vacation like all the magazines right now suggest."

"I guess. The poor bastards probably can't even afford to see the trees. These parks cost a small fortune for the privilege."

Without verbally conceding that their plan was a little uncalled for, the couple threw in the collective towel. Maybe Claire could write a sestina about the experience. Maybe Jack could form a subcommittee on the pros and cons of recreation passes at next month's city meeting. What kind of "Land of the Free" mentality is it, anyway, to ask a man who works fifty weeks a year just to accumulate his two weeks of paid vacation to then spend his money looking at trees. It just wasn't right.

"Yeah, and fuck you, too!" the man yelled at the closest pass of his driver's side window. With a sound like a giant marshmallow lumbering over gravel, the man peeled out of the national park entrance the only way an overloaded RV can.

Claire said, "Looks like it's time we get the band back together." From a woven bag crammed with beach supplies in the back seat, she grabbed her tennis shoes.

"It's on, kid. But what do we do?"

Claire tossed her flimsy espadrilles in the backseat. She hid her salt-and-pepper pedicure under fresh ankle socks with a white pompom attached to the back of each. She laced one of her shoes with a dexterity usually reserved more for athletes than poets. "It depends," she grunted, hunched over, aware of a slight paunch growing larger with each of her Indian lunches.

Jack backed out of the park entrance, a flash of thick brown tree trunk in his review mirror, and followed the RV down the highway, far enough behind to not be obtrusive. "On what?"

"On whether or not we want to get caught."

The husband. The HE of Claire's poems. The man she delineated into a series of parts separated from his Ego and Id by a tenuous line of muscles that didn't quite hold up their youthful promise of virility; by organs, both internal and the one most obvious, the one that didn't pump with as much tenacity anymore. His body tensed next to his wife as Jack drove toward the only campground near their motel.

"I think we missed check-in," he said. "And the fine print said they open the spots to other people on weekends after six."

Claire scribbled in her own small vacation notebook. A quick glance from the shadow-dappled two-lane road ahead revealed a grocery list. Jack saw the words "rope" and "duct tape" written in the familiar bubble doodles she swore resembled Sylvia Plath's handwriting from her Smith College days, when a black hairband held back Plath's dark blonde Veronica Lake bangs and she had no idea who, or what, was coming for her. Jack used to ask his wife, in the earliest days of their relationship, how someone with that girlish bubble writing, as if the exaggerated roundness of each curve could balloon into the kind of cotton-candy thoughts that float in the summer sky, could commit suicide.

"I guess you could call it a compromise," Claire answered. Jack could no more tell then than now when she was joking. "At least she didn't kill Ted Hughes. That's what I would've done."

How could his own wife curve words like "rope" and "duct tape" and "frying pan" across her travel notebook with the same noncommittal smoothness of her wrist, the same veracity of self-assuredness. A blind corner approached as he sped into the fading light.

Jack waited in the car with an erection that surprised him as much as it would surprise her. Claire's order, that he was to wait in the grocery store parking lot to avoid being filmed, together, on one of those shoplift prevention cameras.

The longer Claire took to return, the harder Jack got. This hardness felt unusual in the middle of the day, in the middle of a parking lot, in the middle of his forties; it wasn't necessarily a pleasant feeling, the rush of blood, the familiar swelling, for what he pretended to ignore in the grocery store parking lot while his wife bought duct tape and rope and a four-pack of marshmallow roasting prongs with long-handled metal rods was weighted with fear.

"I probably should've gone to separate check stands to get the tape and the rope, but fuck it." Claire threw her bag and the metal rods in the backseat. She looked around like someone had followed her out of the store.

"Fuck it?" Jack wanted to search through the grocery bag. His wife never spoke that way, even in her sexier poems. His fingers refused to untie the double knot Claire twisted into the plastic bag. The coastal air outside the car mixed with the first smells of campfire. "*Fuck it*, Claire? You're a poet, for Chrissakes. What do you really think we're going to do with duct tape and a rope?"

As much as he protested, Jack's bodily awareness of warmth, eroticism tingling his hidden nerves, built as his wife reached into the bag to show him what she bought.

"It's only licorice shoestrings, silly." She pulled two large bags of coiled candy ropes from the grocery bag. "And they're even red, see?"

Jack felt every ounce of sexual excitement drain back into his body. "Oh. Of course."

"And the tape is for us, and I don't mean to wrap presents."

"But what about the skewers?"

"Do you want to know what really took so long in there? I was making reservations from my phone to stay in the lodge you told me about, you know, near that campground. In fact, the place overlooks the whole area, so we can keep an eye on our vacationing couple while basking in our own private fireplace warmth."

The lodge touted itself as a lavish stop amid the redwoods, where travelers could tuck into real feather beds after dining on flaming Steak Diane and a dry martini or two. The secret watering hole of the Rat Pack all those years ago, a brochure said. Joey Bishop got drunk on Manhattans in their pool. Dean Martin played a tune on the lobby's piano. Someone invented the Kahlua and Cream on a chilly winter night, when Frank and the gang took a break from their standing gig at The Sands to freeze their asses off in peace.

"So we were never really going to teach that awful man a lesson he'd never forget? We weren't even going to scare him a little?"

"You know what, Jack," Claire grabbed his face to pull his lips to hers. They tasted of watermelon gum. He could not remember her ever grabbing his face or ever tasting like watermelon gum. "I say fuck it." She kissed him again. Hard.

The lodge reminded Jack of a horror movie, complete with a lobby check-in man who doubled as the lodge bartender and tripled as the waiter/cook. Taxidermied animals in need of a good bath crowded the lobby walls. Claire investigated the sitting room while Jack paid too much for a corner suite. Board games with missing pieces crowded the sitting room side tables, and Claire made a mental note to steal the backgammon game, made from construction paper glued to the other side of a checkers board. The fabled piano sat in the lobby corner with a layer of dust over even its sign, a crooked three by five card that read Do Not Play.

A quick tour of the room before supper revealed the suite to be an undersized, cold room comprised of a vanity, a fan, and a bed almost too small to have fun in. The couple had their own private bathroom. Jack assumed the toilet flushed.

The restaurant—on their brochure advertising weekend midnight cotillions and mock turtle soup for the first course—closed at six. Steak Diane had disappeared from the menu to be replaced by a club sandwich, a patty melt, and a plate of spaghetti and meatballs with "garlic toast points." Dessert included slices of defrosted Sarah Lee cake cut into thin wedges and garnished with an "artistic swirl of Bosco."

The man who checked them in poured Jack and Claire a Scotch on the rocks after he sat them at a table in the dining room overlooking the campground.

Claire said, "I guess this place has seen better days, but it does retain a certain Old World charm. And how perfect we can see that RV from here."

The waiter brought the couple a bread basket and three pats of butter. Another poem. A poem about sustenance. A poem about the longing for simple carbs. A poem about middle-aged erections, lost and found.

Jack upgraded his patty melt to include tater tots. Claire ordered the club but asked for the bread to be held. From their table they watched the couple set up their own table outside the RV, a private world lit by an incandescence they finally caught up to. As they ate without speaking, Jack and Claire watched the couple lay out picnic supplies. He screwed the gas canister into place and lit the barbecue. She pulled hot dogs from their plastic wrap and handed him each dog with a smile. He nodded at her. She cut up onions. He grated cheese. In a few minutes, the smell of grilled campground hot dogs permeated the dining room.

"It's very picturesque down there," Claire said.

Jack chewed the crispy edge off of a tater tot. He dropped the greasy potato into his ketchup. "I can't believe they hold hands while they eat."

The woman in the campground below piped ketchup onto her husband's hotdog. He returned the gesture by daubing on her dog a line of mustard so electric yellow, Claire wished she had worn sunglasses to dinner.

"Oh, Jack," she said as other couples in the restaurant ordered dessert, "why don't we just get up and walk out of here?"

"What's gotten into you now?" He examined the lodge dessert menu, tried to decide between chocolate or carrot cake. "I know the place is a little more dusty around the edges than the brochure conveyed, but still."

He wanted to add, *and you lured me here under false pretenses. I am trying to make the best of the fact that you don't really want to "teach these people a lesson," like you said, so why don't you back the fuck off.*

"It isn't the lodge and it isn't the food. I pretty much knew a place like this, so far away from everything, wasn't going to be what it promised. It's just that I want to have a picnic with you, right now. Just like they are doing, only better because our picnic will actually mean something."

In late twilight, the campground couple moved with a syncopation few couples master, the grace of movement between lovers earned more than learned. No misplaced motion. No sympathy giggle at the end of a joke fallen flat. No silence, except the quiet that wraps around considering each other.

Claire decided not to order a slice of cake. "I think I hate them," she said.

"Jesus, Claire. We just ate and now you want to have a picnic?"

"Forget the hotdogs, then." Claire stood from the table. No one in the restaurant looked up. People, men, had stopped noticing her a few years before. She didn't know if this pushed her closer to her husband or pulled them farther apart. "Let's make s'mores or something. Let's just walk over there and light a fire right in their faces. We'll show them, for pretending to be so much in love when they really have no idea."

The bartender/waiter/cook wrote the bill's total on an index card he left at the front desk after Jack asked him to charge dinner to their room. He dropped two Andes mints on the dining table. Claire unwrapped both mints at the same time, decided they were too melted to share, and licked each mint off its green paper.

"Come on." She motioned for Jack to follow her to their upstairs room. "Let's grab some stuff. If you're full, we can at least make dessert."

The couple walked up the stairs in a formation they had cultivated and kept since their wedding night, Claire always leading, Jack forced to follow. Always two or three steps behind, the effect in their early marriage was that of Claire becoming the prize Jack struggled to attain. Years of staring at her, always ahead, like the shadow on the sidewalk he could never catch, transformed him from a participant in a sort of game of hide-and-seek to resenting Claire for reaching each destination, and each decision, first.

At the top of the stairs, Jack caught up to his wife. He demanded she hand him their room key.

He didn't respond when she asked, "What's gotten into you all of a sudden?"

Inside the room, the couple fought for dominance to grab the grocery sack. Jack said, "Why don't you let your husband be in charge for a change?"

"You wouldn't even know how." Claire turned her back on Jack to rifle through the sack.

He saw a flash of red licorice ropes. He saw the duct tape she had teased him with, knowing there were no secret sexual moves Claire intended on acting out. Poets only pretend they want someone to tie them up. Jack was tired of pretending. He grabbed Claire.

"Not now, Jack. We're running out of daylight. If we wait too long, that couple won't even see us rubbing our relationship in their faces."

Jack picked up his wife without turning her around. He threw her onto their small lodge bed, his back aching with her weight, slim yet still heavier than the hero in a romance novel ever lets on. The bed creaked, the only sound as Claire held her breath. She looked at Jack like she wanted to scream before all signs of emotion left her face.

She said, "If you're going to act like an animal, then be prepared for me to treat you like one."

Jack pulled off her clothes and discarded them next to the bed. She did not struggle. A button tore from her shirt, the yellow vacation shirt he always thought washed out her olive skin, creating an ugliness he refused to see, let alone comment on. Using the plastic grocery bag, Jack tied Claire's wrists a few feet apart on the brass bed frame.

"Oh my God," she said, flat and unaffected, as if she were studying the scene outside of herself to write about as soon as they got home. "Do you really think something this clichéd is going to turn me on?"

"I don't care if it turns you on."

He placed a small piece of duct tape over Claire's mouth. So she would not feel as scared as she looked when the tape made contact with her lipstick, he stuck a piece of tape over his mouth, too. He motioned to Claire, a question without words, since the couple thought all these years they knew each other so well, if she wanted him, somehow, to tie his wrists to the bedpost, too. She shook her head no. He got on top of her.

Even with their mouths gagged and her wrists bound, sex felt the same at it always did. Not exactly great. Not exactly bad.

After Jack crawled off Claire and swiped a thin hotel hand towel between her legs, he untied her wrists. The couple sat on the bed facing each other with their knees touching. They did not put on clothes. They kept the duct tape on their mouths. This meant no after sex-cigarette or nibble on a red licorice rope. This meant they did not need to talk to each other, did not need to pretend they enjoyed what just happened, or would enjoy it more the next time.

The longer Jack and Claire stared at each other, the more light that vanished outside their lodge room window to reveal stars rising over the forest, the more their eyes watered.

Jack wanted to say to Claire, "Don't cry, sweetheart. It will make you gag."

He thought from the way his wife looked at him, without turning away, that Claire was trying to tell him, "It's okay that I didn't like it."

"Sometimes," he wanted to say back, hoped he said back with his rapid, tear-heavy blinks, "couples just need to compromise."

He stood from the bed to wipe his eyes. Claire followed him. He handed her a tissue to blow her nose. Jack and Claire both wondered if the couple in the RV were making love now, full from their dinner, buying time and churning up more appetite before they toasted marshmallows around a campfire. Jack and Claire refused to stand for it, those people acting like they understood the nuances of love. They were probably newlyweds on their second or third marriage each, rubbing everyone else's nose in so much public fawning.

Jack and Claire stepped back into their clothes. She did not acknowledge the missing button. With duct tape still over their mouths, Jack grabbed a hotdog skewer from the grocery bag and handed the other to Claire. He wondered if the skewer was as sharp as it looked. He wondered what people in love look like when a stranger comes up behind them in the middle of an otherwise ordinary night.

The Borrower

The new neighbor moved in across the street the way Ingrid imagined the Rolling Stones moved into their chateau in the south of France to record *Exile on Main Street,* all chandeliers and drugs. Ingrid tried to distract herself from thinking about Brian and how much he didn't want to have a baby with her by pondering the way her new neighbor flitted from box to moving box as if she heard music inside her head.

"She looks like her own groupie," Ingrid spoke toward the closed living room window.

She knew Brian would be home late, again. He didn't care how hard it was to contort her body each morning to pee on an ovulation predictor stick without peeing on her hand. He didn't care that her body held a ripe egg safe for only three days a month. He tried to pretend he did, but Ingrid knew Brian didn't really care that the little blue line appeared that morning.

"Look at her. So young and clueless. She probably has enough eggs left, and enough boyfriends, to never have to worry about something like this."

The unnatural blonde, who wore a short velvet capelet in the middle of June, directed movers to clip the twine on large, thin packages hiding rococo mirrors, squat boxes that held claw-footed buffet tables. Chandeliers splayed their crystal arms across the lawn. By mid-afternoon, the clouds revealed a sun that emphasized each hand-cut prism until the new neighbor's yard undulated like some mythical underwater sea creature.

Again Ingrid thought of drugs as she stared from her living room window, then at the desk where she was supposed to sit and finish a final edit on a gluten-free cookbook. Her edits tracked across the document in emphatic red lines like lines of coke on a mirror. Lines of coke on a mirror? Ingrid had never thought about cocaine in her entire life. Why was she thinking of cocaine now, on a very ordinary Tuesday afternoon at the edge of a suburban neighborhood? And would the egg her body readied again this month wait until Brian was ready? She'd already gone through this whole menstruating thing since she was twelve and started bleeding in the school bathroom. Twenty-five years meant three hundred chances to have a baby. Maybe three hundred and one would finally turn her into the goose that laid the golden egg, or something close enough to buy baby books and a silver rattle and a diaper genie.

Ingrid tried to stop thinking about becoming a mother, at thirty-seven, and focus on the book by an author in the stable of authors at the mid-range publishing company where she had edited long enough, and with the least amount of to-press errors, to work from home.

"You're wasting your time editing cookbooks when you should really be designing a nursery. And I saw you watching me," a voice purred behind her left ear.

Ingrid turned to see her new neighbor sitting on the couch in her living room without appearing to have opened, or closed, the front door. Sitting wasn't even the right word for the way the woman arranged herself on the sofa as if this object, or any object she came close enough to touch, became regal in her presence.

"I'm Sheba."

Sheba with a face like the face in an old-fashioned perfume ad, cheekbones appled and high nose upturned and pinched. Lips red and small and smiling in a way that Ingrid told herself someone with a more average job than editing a bestselling cookbook might see as threatening.

"I'm Ingrid."

Sheba ignored Ingrid's attempt to say hello, to surface from the underbelly of her very ordinary body and face. She pointed to a paper plate piled with cookies, which sat next to her on the couch. "You're going to need a little help, so I made these for you," she said between draws on a cigarette secure in a thin black holder with a gold tip. "Oh, forgive my faux pas. I know it's much too early in the day to smoke from an opera length, but I must've lost my cocktail length in the move. And I saw you watching me, like I said." The living room filled with soft currents of pleasant-smelling smoke. Ingrid felt a little faint. "You will need these cookies tonight."

"Tonight?" Ingrid couldn't help but draw closer. She sat down tentatively between the strange new neighbor and her paper plate.

"Go ahead, love. Try one." With her free hand, Sheba unrolled the film of cellophane that covered the cookies as if she was unveiling a new piece of art. Beneath the clear wrapping sat a sugary mound of what looked like butter cookies. "But these are no ordinary butter cookies," she said, as if reading Ingrid's thoughts, cellophane shredded in a hypnotizing pattern from the pressure of Sheba's red manicure. "These cookies are magic."

"Magic? You really are on drugs, aren't you?" Ingrid asked. She felt awkward at not having offered her guest something to drink, or to hang up her velvet capelet.

"You're sweet." Sheba picked up a cookie imprinted with what looked like a man's profile. It could have been Brian's.

"Are you already after my husband? Is that what this is all about? Because if you are, trust me, he isn't worth it."

"Just try one. You'll see." Sheba leaned against the couch cushion like an indolent animal with no threat of a cage anywhere in sight, tamed only by the cigarette holder. From Ingrid's angle it cut her pale face in two.

It had been a frustrating day, or maybe a boring day, or maybe, even worse, a day like any other of Ingrid's days. Edit work in the morning, a break for a yogurt at noon, turkey sandwich at one, followed by more editing until Brian got home and the couple could stop working to focus on their cell phones the rest of the night. A completely ordinary day, except for the little blue line alerting Ingrid that her body was ready to make her a mom.

"I hate to be personal with someone I just met, but no matter how good your cookies may be—and don't get me wrong, they do look glamorous..." Ingrid stared at the plate, star shapes and ovals and complicated spirals turning in on each other, topped with golden glitter. "...they still can't fix what's wrong in this house."

Sheba stood from the couch with a star-shaped cookie in her creamy hand. Pink fingernails like childhood bubblegum right out of the wrapper, Ingrid thought. "Yes, they were red a moment ago. I changed them after you decided in your mind that the color looked too threatening."

"I make it a point to never trust a woman with red fingernails."

"That's fair."

"And you are very different from the other neighbors." Ingrid tugged at her brown sweater. Her clothes never fit her body the way they fit the bodies of women in catalogs. She longed to wear velvet the way Sheba wore velvet.

"These cookies will make your deepest desire come true, but they do come at a price. I believe in full disclosure." Sheba asked Ingrid to open her mouth, and Ingrid opened with an obedience reserved for her husband in the early years of their marriage, when she thought he could do no wrong. "If you use these cookies in the way they are intended, I may ask for something in return."

"I don't think I have anything you could possibly want."

"One never knows." Sheba placed the cookie on Ingrid's tongue. "Before you bite down, do we have an agreement?"

"Yes, we do."

A feeling of religiosity flooded Ingrid, the same feeling she recalled from noon mass in Catholic school. Yet the sacrament of the Eucharist never felt so exciting, or like it held the possibility of leading to such trouble. It wasn't so much what she tasted that transported her into a dream or a fantasy, she could not tell, but what she saw as she closed her eyes and the cookie dissolved.

Brian stood before her, the vision of him a little milky around the edges, as if someone had dipped her husband in whitewash. Beyond the white edging, though, Ingrid heard her husband's laughter, the way he used to laugh before the backbeat of remorse that follows a long marriage. In the vision Ingrid laughed, too, as if she and her husband were in on some great, mesmerizing secret, the sort of secret only lovers keep between themselves, never husbands and wives.

"We definitely have an agreement," she said after surfacing from the secure blanket of imagined laughter. But Sheba was gone, and twilight blued the edges of the room in a way Ingrid almost felt frightened of until she reprimanded herself. "Now you're just being silly," she said to the foyer mirror.

A little woozy, Ingrid steadied herself when she stood from the couch. She wondered if this feeling was the feeling wild women have carried with their lipsticks and compacts through history. Head spinning, heart missing every third beat, her feet were unable to keep up with each other. She felt like a bad girl coming home the next morning in the clothes she went out in the night before. She loved the disheveled way her hair favored one shoulder, the sudden hunger that compelled her to eat large scoops of macaroni salad from the fridge with her hands. She downed two yogurts, their cups crushed like frat-party beer cans she tossed on the kitchen floor. Leftover spaghetti she dangled toward her mouth, sauced ends leaving greasy red marks around her lips.

When she finally felt full enough to close the refrigerator door—not satiated, only less starved—she went back to the living room and placed the plate of Sheba's cookies on the foyer table next to the day's unopened mail. Her husband never said hello, or even acknowledged Ingrid's existence, until he went through every catalog and bill. Even on day's with the blue ovulation line.

"Hon?" she said when, from the kitchen, she heard Brian open the door and head for the bills. The term of endearment usually caused her husband to surface from his murky after-work malaise of questioning purchases on the credit card statement he chased around his palms like a fresh-caught fish, his weak attempt to feign shock as their debt grew.

The foyer always dropped into silence right before Brian's nightly lesson about the importance of Ingrid sticking to a budget. Where was his admonition for her to, please, just this once try to spend a little less? Ingrid heard nothing but the silent yet burgeoning pleasure of a just-eaten butter cookie. She peeked around the kitchen island, and in the foyer mirror caught the reflection of her husband's mouth stuffed with cookies.

He still loves me, we can still keep this going, even for a little while longer, Ingrid thought as Brian stretched his arms toward her. They embraced in a slow, clumsy waltz. The front hall spun away from them in leisurely circles, the cookbook manuscript blinking for help inside her computer. The hall clock stopped ticking as the couple touched each other for the first time as this novel, mysterious version of their former selves. Brian didn't ask if Ingrid baked the cookies, or even mention that every cookie from the stash placed in his suit pocket, beneath the star shapes and the ovals and hearts, resembled his wife somehow. Talking about something so wonderful might ruin the magic, and the newly shy lovers vowed to never waste another moment wondering about the details, or the unnatural blonde devil Ingrid sensed, yet refused to see, hiding deep inside.

"Maybe I could take that silver cup I saw on the fireplace mantle? Or your grandfather clock? The last grandfather clock I owned never kept time. I told Mr. Clement his royal pendulum swung at two seconds instead of one, but when would a man who made clocks ever listen to a woman like me?"

Sheba let herself in the next morning after Brian went to work, neither he or Ingrid remembering much about the night before, except the feeling of happiness and the final note of the perfume she only wore during sex hanging stale in the morning air. They woke up stunned to have caught, and kept safe, the fickle and precious and rare little bird the couple, in their now quiet, gentle way, agreed to coddle into a great passion between them. A bond too powerful for even the weight of their former wedding vows to diminish.

"The thing is," Sheba sat on the side table next to the kitchen, filing her fingernails, "clocks always stop around me. But this time, new place, new friends, maybe I'll get lucky? Oh, you noticed my *lime à ongles.*" She motioned to the thin grey pencil-shaped board she moved over each nail. "Marie gave this to me before she passed."

"Marie?"

"Antoinette. And to think the poor thing never even told anyone they should eat cake. Between you and me, though, she was still kind of a bitch, excuse my French." Ingrid struggled to make coffee without putting her contacts in first. "Now you're talking crazy," she said, spilling coffee beans across the counter, though she knew Sheba was telling the truth.

"Did you know Marie made her chambermaids wash this file every night to be ready for her the next morning? It shows you what kind of queen she really was, filing her nails every single day like that." Ingrid ignored Sheba the way sisters ignore each other. She struggled to remember everything about the night before, about Brian, about her blue line, but her mind couldn't recall a single thing, except the taste of Sheba's cookies. She imagined the feeling to be similar to those people who are always late or never turn in their edits on time or burn every dinner but show up to their life with that goofy, nonchalant look. Ingrid roiled around in the pleasure, as the coffee water boiled, of experiencing one morning of her life where she just let things happen, including waking up to find Sheba dressed in silk pajamas and doing her nails.

"I think Marie was lucky, getting to live as spoiled as she was for as long as she did. Petit Trianon, anyone? Come on. And, my love, you must know most things revolve around luck, but not all things."

Ingrid watched Sheba, transfixed, her cool hands warming around her coffee as Sheba made herself up in the foyer mirror. From a small beaded purse that changed from silver to gold when pencils of sunlight scribbled through the French doors, Sheba pulled out a white stick that looked like a crayon. Wherever she touched the crayon to her face, her complexion paled like a statue.

"I can do it lighter, or darker, if you like?"

A line of compacts and tiny jeweled bottles took up most of the space on the end table reserved for the day's mail. With liquid movement—like a pale wave overtook her house, receded, then came back again and again, with more force each time—the new neighbor before the mirror snapped her fingers to change her hair color from the darkest brunette to almost white to red more like nail polish than any color found on a human head. Next Sheba chose green eyes.

"Eyes like Rita Hayworth," she said to the mirror, though Ingrid didn't exactly know who Rita Hayworth was beyond an actress from black-and-white movies her grandmother used to watch.

"I really am sorry I don't have anything better to offer you. But," Ingrid paused with a long sip of coffee, "what dream of mine came true that I owe you anything at all?"

"I really have to tweak my recipe a bit. It's disconcerting to us both, your loss of memory. It makes the rest of our transaction seem so, well, messy. And you're right, the cup isn't the greatest, and Brian would definitely notice a missing grandfather clock. What about that blue vase I saw on the upstairs hall table?"

"You've been upstairs?" With tissues Ingrid wiped the makeup smears Sheba left across the foyer table. She swallowed more coffee, but the aftertaste made her gag. "I don't remember showing you around up there."

"I popped in late last night for a jiff. You two were really going at it." Sheba made an obscene gesture with her perfectly manicured hands. A ring of precious gemstones wrapped around each of her fingers and thumbs.

Going at it? Us? Really? Of course she recalled the cookies, could still actually taste the butter melting in her mouth, and that unusual herbal aftertaste she could not place, and how, if she thought of it, the sensation almost came back. She nearly felt dizzy. She held onto the coat rack. Had she and Brian made love? How could she forget something as monumental as having sex with her husband, when she was fertile, in the middle of the week, without being on vacation? In a daze she grabbed the silver cup off the mantle. She tried to hand the cup to Sheba

Sheba refused the cup with a graceful wave of her hand. Every time she moved, perfume weighted the air. "No, love, you were right before. You have no idea how many of these I already have."

"But nothing else I own has any value. What would someone like you want with any of my knickknacks or souvenirs, anyway?"

"Don't you worry about that." Sheba leaned in close to Ingrid, close enough to almost rub her hands across Ingrid's stomach. From the corner of her eye, Ingrid thought she saw a dark little forked tongue flick from the new neighbor's mouth. When she looked again, she saw Sheba smiling at her with pretty pink lips. "We have a good nine months to figure something out."

Just the Right Kind
of Stranger

The Human Resources department, which in Irene's office consisted of Janet moving her chair into a spare room with a door that locked, called Irene in for a farewell "talk."

"Do you know why we're letting you go?" Janet asked. She fidgeted with a stray curl frizzing from the air conditioning. Under the lights, Irene thought the woman's skin looked the color of lemonade.

"Your skin looks really yellow. Are you not feeling well?"

She and Janet had the kind of work history that went back far enough to track a migratory route across their town and two towns over. They had donated enough money for each other's birthday cakes and signed enough of each other's passed-around birthday cards to become honorary acquaintances. Irene brought a paper bag or two of zucchini to Janet every summer from her own backyard. Janet told Irene when upper management considered her lipstick too "garish." Irene told Janet when her skin looked like lemonade. There might be a lot more to other friendships, but there could also be a lot less.

"I feel fine. And we aren't here to talk about me." Janet's stray curl sprang back into the dark brown mass.

"I only mentioned your skin because I would want you to do the same for me."

Janet used her scuffed brown pumps to push her chair backward over the industrial carpet. Irene stood. She would have stared out the window, if there was one. She wondered if people only get fired in rooms without windows.

Again Janet asked, "Do you know why we are letting you go?"

"If you want me to be honest," Irene said, trying to block any concern for the jaundice that yellowed her friend's cheeks, "I didn't know anyone *was* letting me go."

"You've received both written and emailed memos."

Irene did not like the way Janet stared at the barely discernible houndstooth pattern stamped on the carpet instead of at her own non-yellow face.

"So," Janet continued, "since you seem to be unresponsive?"

Unresponsive? Irene pondered the word, wished she had a background in Latin, wished she knew the difference between a suffix and a prefix, wished she knew why Janet sounded like such a total bitch, this woman who had even told her the secret ingredient in her county fair blue-ribbon-winning recipe for zucchini bread. (Don't tell anyone, but it all hinged on crushed pineapple.)

Janet stopped shuffling her shoes across the houndstooth. "We're letting you go because you won't stop asking your fellow employees, all male, if they have ever considered abducting you."

"That's a lie." Irene stared at the wall where a window should be. "I only asked one or two of them."

"There were five at last count."

"Okay, so I asked five men who work here if they consider me alluring enough to abduct. You know," Irene pushed her own unruly curls behind her ears, "like, am I alluring enough for a killer to kill or a rapist to rape—that sort of thing."

"Mr. Shields asked me to inform you we will send your personal effects to your home. You are to leave the premises immediately and, as a personal favor," Janet scooted her chair closer to Irene, "I ask that you never add crushed pineapple to your zucchini bread from this point forward."

"Don't worry," Irene said. "I'll never let a man abduct me after luring him out from whichever rock he's hiding under with a lump of your dry, shitty bread."

"Do you really think it's dry?" Janet asked as Irene left the room, not turning around to answer her new ex-friend. She heard Janet yell from the hallway, "Did you remember to add the buttermilk?"

A perverse thrill tingled through Irene. Fired! In movies, the boss only fires the resident badass, the person who knows too much, talks with too much poise, orders pre-stirred yogurt to be served at breakfast meetings instead of the more affordable brand with fruit at the bottom. She caught the down elevator, feeling elated for the short ride to the employee parking garage.

"If they think there's something wrong with wanting to be tantalizing enough to abduct, then screw them," Irene said in the parking garage while she tried to remember where she'd parked.

At home, Irene got out of her car in the driveway with the intention of never driving again. In her mind, driving a car would only get in the way of her complete commitment to become vulnerable in a crowd, her vow, to herself, to be in the worst places at the worst times, on foot, alone. One could call this proof Irene carried a death wish. For Irene, though, her desire focused less on wanting to be abducted and more on wanting to feel worthy of abduction.

She knew, after reading every true crime book and watching all the television biographies, that some killers have a "type" and will never deviate, even if Marilyn Monroe or, in this day, Miley Cyrus walked naked into their arms. Brown hair parted down the middle, blonde curls, bangs or no bangs, petite, fat—Irene crossed these specifics off her list. She needed to be abducted by a person with no pattern, a garden-variety sociopath who hated his mother. Even in the small town where she lived and now didn't work, a man like that shouldn't be too hard to find.

Reading self-help books in her spare time, which became all the time, taught Irene that in order to achieve a goal, one must go after that goal with fierce determination. One of the seven highly effective habits.

After a long weekend contemplating where to look for a job—Janet was clear none of Irene's prospective new employers were to call for a reference—Irene woke on Monday morning with what felt to her like a highly effective habit.

"I know how to lure a man to me," she said to her empty bedroom. "It's not like we haven't been luring men to us since Eve knew Adam would find her more appealing after she ate the apple."

Her room, like her small house, gave off the appearance of a chronically single woman. The type of woman, in her early thirties, who was ripe for abduction, not too old yet to be seen by most predators as obsolete. Irene had the obligatory cat, named Cat, the sticky Ben & Jerry's containers on her bedroom side tables, a twin bed frosted in shabby chic pillows and sheets, a box of tampons on the bathroom cupboard, no attempt made to hide her body's bloodier secrets from a male companion.

"And it's not like whoever abducts me is going to bring me back here," she said after her morning stretch, Cat petting, and half container of yogurt, which she ate while sitting in the lotus position on top of her bed. With each pale yellow bite, she thought vaguely of suicide. Nothing as tangible as noose tying or pill taking, but if she was really able to channel her desires into reality, what happened after she got abducted? Would she be raped? Brutalized? Murdered?

"I guess the devil really is in the details," she told Cat through a mouthful of lemon yogurt. "I'll figure out the rest of them when it happens. Once whoever takes me realizes I was only putting myself in danger to see what would happen, he'll let me go with a warning." Her cat kneaded Irene's bare thigh. Tiny welts raised on her skin. "I think everyone deserves one warning in life, don't you?"

But remember that one time you thought that, and he didn't stop? Didn't give you a warning, and you wore that dress, the dress that fit you the way none of your other dresses fit, and it wasn't enough to tell you he really loved your dress? None of it was enough. But that was isolated, unreported, and not every man who is like that is like that, right?

In her small kitchen, Irene assembled, on a counter not much bigger than her sink, the ingredients to make one perfect cupcake. Ever since the second *Sex in the City* movie, where they show Charlotte crying inside a pantry stocked with shelves of sprinkles and edible luster dust, Irene sought to replicate the well-off character's pantry, albeit one she moved through her kitchen by lugging around the pantry around in a large shoebox. Sprinkles stuck to the bottom of the box where a food coloring spill made a yellow-orange Rorschach. Dragées, powdered royal icing, a rolled sheet of fondant—everything waited for Irene to create a cupcake worthy of attracting the wrong kind of attention.

"Look here, Cat, at the trap I'm setting."

Wasn't baking really a sort of unspoken female alchemy, after all? Boxes of cookies sent to the troops? That apple pie the teen Cutter daughter was so very good at baking for her boyfriend that the details made their way into Capote's book?

"But nobody eats pie anymore," Irene said as she constructed a scant golden batter to pour into one muffin cup, nestled in the center of her muffin pan.

She waited in front of the oven for her cupcake to rise and turn golden brown. Feeling in a hurry, after the cake cooled she frosted it with store-bought icing. A heavy hand of sprinkles and Irene set off, dressed in her jogging suit, for the park closest to the lake that skimmed her town.

No one in her town's history had reported an abduction anywhere near the murky lake that congealed with debris each winter. Still, the lake conjured the kind of nightmares that invaded the mind of every local teenage girl. It was the kind of lake no one would be surprised to see a news van parked beside. The kind of lake Frankenstein's monster might drown little Marie in.

Not much for jogging, Irene speed-walked the length of the gravel path rimming the lake's edge. Other women with smaller thighs jogged past her. Some even turned to look at the single cupcake she carried on a paper plate.

"It's not for me!" she yelled at the back of a bouncing blonde ponytail. "It's for him!"

But how would any man, predator or not, notice her among all the young things sparkling in their pink spandex like flashes of a succulent new fruit unpeeling itself?

Irene left the main trail for a forest path that looped deeper into the woods. The lake bracken with its raw sewage undertone disappeared from her tunnel vision, replaced by a dense forest and even darker monsters. The paper plate shook as she trotted along a path absent of any tennis shoe tracks—but the shaking was excitement, she told herself, never fear. Fear was for women who refused to live on the edge.

"And I will never be that kind of woman," she said to the cupcake. The sugar glitter created rainbow prisms when sunlight hit the buttercream.

Hours into her walk, Irene's feet hurt. She had wandered around the lake perimeter and the darkest of woods, way out of the park boundaries with the cheerful children and the weekly puppet show. Her cupcake began to wilt. No matter how long she waited—past mid-afternoon, when Irene assumed men took late lunch breaks from their downtown offices in search of women to abduct; past twilight, which Janet with the lemonade skin called the *gloaming* because she saw the word once in a novel— no men came.

Irene trekked through the woods back to her car while the sun dropped fast, the only light in the bluing perimeter the reflection of her vanilla cupcake and the paper plate, a sugary beacon she held at arm's length to light the way home.

She and Cat shared the cupcake on top of her bed. Sprinkles covered her thick white comforter, got caught on the ends of Cat's whiskers, as if she and her pet threw a party but forgot all the details as soon as the last guest left.

"Maybe what I need are mini cupcakes?"

Cat stared at Irene as if he wondered what would happen if his owner never came back.

"Remember that time I went walking in the snow?" she asked her pet. Irene preheated the oven. Soon, batter filled a mini muffin pan. "Well, of course you don't really remember. It's not like I took you with me. I would if I thought you'd enjoy it, but this walk in the woods was more of a solo journey, one of those soul-searching, partly mystical moments."

Irene used a rubber spatula to add softened butter to her mixer: making frosting from scratch this time, measuring the powdered sugar by eye. The sound of her mixer reminded her of what Cat might sound like amplified.

"I remember a few years ago, when you disappeared for a week. Janet offered to make flyers. Little did I know she would have immediately reported me to Human Resources for using company supplies for personal business." She stuck her finger in the frosting. "Too much sugar!" After thinning the frosting with flavored coffee creamer, a secret she'd never told, even after Janet shared her zucchini bread recipe, she said, "But I knew you were out doing what you felt you needed to do, and that it was none of my business. Just like when I went walking in the snow. Janet, and even the other women at work, the ones who found it more interesting to talk *at* me about the latest episode of *Modern Family* though they know I don't own a television, warned me about walking in the snow."

You might trip and fall, Irene, knowing you.

I'm not using my lunch break to drive you to the Immediate Care.

And we won't take contributions for a Get Well Fund, either.

"But I needed to walk alone in the snow. It was because of the murder. Months after they found the woman's body, and months before her husband confessed as part of a sentencing agreement. All I know is that when I think about that walk, I still feel happy."

Irene's cat stared at the mini cupcakes rising in their suitably diminutive polka-dot baking cups.

"The place where I walked looked like something out of a greeting card. I felt like God gave me the gift of being the only one in our entire town to trek through untouched snow, to accept my destiny without question. I have lived my entire life, like all women live, afraid that something bad is going to happen to me. Well, you know what? I'm not afraid anymore."

The oven timer alerted Irene that her mini cupcakes were ready for their own flour and sugar destiny.

After a fitful sleep, tossing enough that Cat moved from his customary position next to her, Irene woke ready for phase two. She dressed in a business suit. Her "I mean business suit," as Janet once called the ensemble, while the two women shared a tuna fish sandwich and criticized every article in *O Magazine*.

"She's so out of touch," Irene remembered Janet saying, "with her celebrity friends and their gluten-free barbecue."

"All barbecue is gluten-free," Irene answered. She liked how Janet spiked her tuna salad with sweet pickle relish.

Someday she would make a tuna salad sandwich with sweet pickle relish and not give Janet any credit.

"You know what I mean. And you know I know what real women—not Gwyneth Paltrow—want better than stupid Oprah does."

But Janet had no clue, Irene thought as she ran a lint brush over her navy-blue lapels. And she never will. She arranged the cupcakes on a plastic tray, all but the one she placed in Cat's bowl of kitty chow.

A plastic serving tray of cupcakes would always catch the attention of children. They followed her through the park as Irene headed toward the lake for the second day in a row. In her business suit and matching pumps, she outran all but two young boys, to whom she tossed cupcakes for their tenacity. At a private cranny where no one but Irene dared to duck out of the implicit safety of sunshine, she placed her first bite-sized morsel. She told herself to work quickly, before moles stole the cupcakes by coaxing them underground with their sleight-of-hand tunnel building.

"Quiet," she told herself as she decorated low-hanging branches with cupcakes. On a thin strip of meadow near the lake's edge, she placed cupcakes that looked like flowers, then stood back to admire her singular determination. "This just has to get a pervert's attention."

Irene tucked her body into a sanctuary of pine needles in a small grove of trees and waited. By nightfall, she lost sight of her own handiwork under the moonless sky. "This is nothing close to a fairy tale," she said. "Especially without a moon to lead my destiny to me, like Hansel's breadcrumbs."

The phrase "like Hansel's breadcrumbs" repeated in her head over and over. This sometimes happened to Irene, born with a brain that stuck in the same track like a record needle in its groove.

"Like Hansel's breadcrumbs?" she questioned the near-dark. "Why does he get all the credit? He's the one that got his dumbass self on the witch's radar in the first place."

Irene didn't know if her epiphany, or series of epiphanies, came from finally acknowledging the world's injustices after a long evening watching every man who jogged through the park ignore her cupcakes—some more suspicious than others, wearing darker sunglasses despite the twilight, some with their beer bellies undulating beneath body-conscious Lycra. She was sick of waiting for the town predator, whom she assumed was out there somewhere, breathing heavy, to tell her, by his brutal and specific interest, that she was worthy of adoration.

Unlike the usual women who starred in missing person posters in her state, Irene was neither blonde nor under thirty. She baked her own birthday cakes from scratch. She came from a long line of Polish descendants complete with premature dowager's humps. She didn't watch *The Real Housewives*. She didn't knit ironic scarves covered in handlebar moustaches. But what set Irene apart more than the missing or the mutilated, the Peggys and Sarahs and Beth-Anns, was how, from that night onward, she wasn't going to wait around for a psychopath's approval.

Pine needles poked holes through her business nylons, the overpriced designer pair Janet had talked her into buying at Macy's. Irene stood to brush the dust from her suit. She'd lost sight of the cupcakes. "Men don't even eat cupcakes," she told herself as her spine cracked back into alignment. She felt the warning tingle of her sciatic nerve. "Men never eat cupcakes. In fact, men think eating a cupcake will make them look 'gay,' whatever being gay looks like. And men who abduct women are probably too lost in their own sickness to notice cupcakes on the ground."

On her march out of the depths of the park, careful to miss most of the benches without a stumble, Irene wondered if silver fox Keith Morrison would ever interview her on a *Dateline Saturday Night Mystery*. She imagined her outfit, her tasteful honey-amber highlights, the way the news anchor would not reveal whether Irene sat in a jail cell or was the story's victim until the last five minutes. She wondered if he ate energy bars, Keith, who looked so fit but so thin. She made a mental note to ask if he made his own granola.

At home, Irene threw away her mini muffin pan. Upended in the kitchen trash, the pan looked more like a part from a spacecraft than an element in what Irene still saw as the extreme act of seduction. Since puberty she had longed to be the victim of a crime of passion. Nancy to her Sid Vicious. That blonde Playboy model to the boyfriend who shot both her and himself. The other blonde woman and whatever Phil Spector did that night in a mansion built on pop songs.

She asked Cat why the weirdoes of the world always go for blondes. Cat slept his feline sleep beside her. "I hope you're ready for a busy day tomorrow, because things are going to start changing around here."

The thin line between love and hate is no thinner, or harder to cross, than the equivalent distance between predator and prey.

"Maybe Janet is right about all those boring self-empowerment books she reads in the break room. Why am I letting someone else control my life when, with just a few tweaks, I can control theirs? Sorry, Cat," she whispered as he slept, "but that means no more cats in my future."

Irene did not cry as much as she thought she would as she boxed up Cat's things the next morning, his bendy stick with the powder-blue feather attached to the end, his scratching post, kibble bowl, favorite blanket. At the shelter, Cat refused to look at Irene when she surrendered him, kennel and all, to a worker. Irene assumed the shelters were like any other place, and that rumors between the cats and the dogs would spread quick enough to knock Cat off his self-important perch. Irene traded him for a pit bull, the dream dog of every aggressive American male.

She hated pit bulls, with their cold eyes, their inability to ever look hospitable, the way boys with too many tattoos, who either sold or took too many drugs, claimed them as a favorite breed. She hated pit bulls because she was afraid of pit bulls, even a spayed female named Molly.

On the way back to her house, over the last sad thought of Cat alone in a world that now teetered between adoption and euthanasia, Irene stared at Molly between breaks in traffic. Molly stared straight ahead, her chocolate brown coat dull and menacing. Molly looked like she wanted to eat the seat cushion but restrained herself just yet. As a plus, she either didn't seem to notice or didn't acknowledge that Irene was on her period. (She remembered the story about a dog attack in San Francisco. Hadn't Keith Morrison said the woman in the hallway was menstruating?)

The dog made herself at home in Irene's small house the way uninvited guests never seem to notice when they eat the last piece of cake. Irene did not speak to Molly the way she spoke to Cat. Her goals had not turned her into a cruel person, or even a person who changed that much. A former friend like Janet would lie in the papers, if anything bad ever happened, about how Irene was a "strange shadow of her former self."

The next morning, Irene ate her daily yogurt cup while sitting cross-legged on top of her bedspread. Molly was not invited. Though her plan demanded drastic action, she allowed herself one sentimental thought about Cat now and then.

"So, what would attract a man?" She directed the question to some invisible and unfelt force around her bedroom. "And I don't mean that," she said to her own reflection in the mirror.

What would cause a man, or at least her type of man, to be drawn out of his own safe warren—maybe only a few doors down, maybe across town—to seek her out instead of all the other waiting women?

A pit bull. Check.

Beef jerky. Mixed nuts. Beer. NCAA March Madness brackets. As Irene gathered what she began to refer to in her head as *man sundries*, she realized she knew nothing about what men really liked. She'd had a string of short-term romances, lean on actual romance. She remembered the sommelier who dumped her because of an "underdeveloped palate" and the college history instructor who said "demarcation line" and "empirical data" at least twice over every dinner, then ignored the "empirical data" that she did not like to go down on him, no matter how nonchalantly he moved her head toward the crotch of his pants. Sometimes there were sweet moments ruined by an ill-timed joke from either member of each shaky duo, or even sweet relationships that inevitably fizzled from what Irene took to calling "Over Under Syndrome." One of the couple was always oversexed or undersexed. Overcommunicated or undercommunicated, was under or over-read in the Classics, under or overweight. Under or overenthusiastic. But Irene knew, even with a string of poor choices, that a man who abducts women could never be under-committed.

"And isn't it a little sad that's what I thought it took to feel special?" she said out loud while hundreds of NCAA March Madness bracket templates shot out of the printer onto the floor. "One bag of beef jerky and a six-pack of beer will not even coax a fifteen-year-old boy my way. I need to make a bigger statement—something so big the local news will bring their van to my front door. Molly," she said, addressing the dog for the first time, "do you know anything about handcuffs? Real ones, not the sex store kind?"

At the bank, Irene emptied her savings account. She spent the rest of the early afternoon filling a grocery cart with cases of beef jerky and cans of mixed nuts, the premium mix with less than forty percent peanuts. She bought enough beer to fill a separate cart three times. Her impulse purchases included a few jars of hot sauce, cans of chili, a box of cheese crackers, and, at the adult store near the off-ramp closest to her house, a pair of those red plastic handcuffs complete with a heart-shaped key.

At home, she fed Molly a small stick of beef jerky. She offered the meat to her new, silent companion without looking at her big, blocky head, a head any man couldn't help but both fear and pet. Janet, back when they were friends, always told Irene, perpetually single and with too much zucchini bread left over, to go on Craigslist to find a man, almost as if the phrase "going on Craigslist" indicated a seismic shift in both attitude and outcome.

Irene sat down in front of her computer to post an ad on Craigslist in the Help Wanted category. She knew from that one *Lifetime* movie about the guy who killed prostitutes he found on Craigslist that she couldn't mention anything sexual, like how she intended to handcuff the first man who showed up at her door, whether or not he looked like her type. She couldn't decide whether to handcuff him to her bed post or the shower rod.

A wave of emotion she could only identify as hatred warmed her torso as Irene sat in front of the blinking cursor. Was this how it felt, to be one of those men on the hunt for a victim? Irene found it almost impossible to reconcile her feelings aimed, almost beyond her control, at a man she hadn't even met yet, the man her subconscious blamed for every failed attempt to feel special throughout her life. And she couldn't decide how to explain in her ad, that box flashing at the bottom of her computer screen, that only a very short time before she had spent what felt like her entire life waiting to be noticed.

After several false starts, Irene erased words like "empowerment" and "prey turned predator" and even "I will be the director for this new crime of passion," and typed:

"Looking for a Hansel to compliment Gretel. Seeking brotherly type to help with various home improvements. Must be strong in both body and spirit and understand how to lead a woman out of the forest of her own making with more than just breadcrumbs. Payment for services."

Irene included a recent picture from a day her YouTube makeup tutorials finally came together. As she waited for the ad to be approved and go "live," Irene gathered up the brackets and the man sundries and went outside. The waning afternoon sun warmed her as she found a stepladder next to the garden hose on the side of the house. She was not used to carrying tools, but enjoyed the feeling of lugging around something more significant than a box filled with baking sugar. Molly waited inside, her curious wet nose pressed against the front door glass as Irene arranged sticks of beef jerky on the side of her front door. She alternated a line of beer cans and bottles down her front porch. On the stepladder, Irene balanced while she stuck row after row of basketball brackets to her roof, the parts she could reach, by first squeezing a layer of hot sauce along the gutter. In a women's magazine, Irene once read how the smell of cinnamon rolls can give men erections. She questioned her choice of beef jerky. She contemplated sprinkling cinnamon in her hair.

"I'm thinking a house of gingerbread must've been a real chore," she said as neighbors slowed their cars to observe Irene's handiwork, cheese crackers and roasted cashews arranged in mosaic patterns down her eaves and around window frames. "I should've bought spray cheese. That would've held the brackets in place better than hot sauce. Oh well, you live and you learn."

A man about her age approached Irene as she placed the last peanut on the last barren spot near her doorframe. "There," she said, her doorframe covered in beef jerky and mixed nuts and crackers and enough college brackets to almost resemble the door in Irene's grown-up version of a fairy tale, "done!"

"Uh, excuse me. I'm here to answer your ad."

Irene turned to gaze at the man. His hair color, build, and general disposition did not register to her. Not even his words felt like they connected to any thought, no matter how hidden or diabolical rolling around in her brain. "That was fast. How did you know where I live?" she asked, brushing peanut crumbs off her pant legs.

"You posted your address."

"I did? Are you sure?"

"Yes, very. And you look a little yellow. Are you feeling okay?" the man asked.

Faceless. Nameless. Just the right kind of stranger.

"I'm the one who's supposed to notice whether or not someone looks yellow."

"I'm sorry. I think I should go." The man backed away. She saw Molly from the corner of her eye, nose still pressed against the glass. "I don't know what's come over me. It's been a rough couple of days, what with just losing my job and then not being able to find a man in town to abduct me."

"Abduct you?" The man stepped closer to Irene. He bent down to place a fallen peanut back in its hot sauce mortar around the doorframe. "That sounds nuts."

"Nuts!" Irene laughed as she pointed to the peanut the stranger had just rearranged. "Now who's nuts?"

The man laughed.

"Listen, if you come inside and help me with a few of the things I mentioned in the ad, I can tell you a story you might not ever believe."

"Well, actually..." The man hesitated at the front door before following Irene past the threshold and deep into her darkened living room. "The ad never mentioned what you need done. But I get the feeling it's something more than I thought. And did you say in the ad your name is Gretel?"

"I think you might be just who I've been waiting for," Irene said as she led the man past Molly, who didn't even look up, toward the bedroom and the handcuffs and the little key molded to mirror her hopeful heart. "And I'm not Gretel, silly. I'm the witch. Just wait until I show you all the things I've been waiting for someone to show me. Just wait."

These stories originally appeared, sometimes in different form, in the following publications: *The Chicago Tribune* ("Selfie" and "Best of Show"), *Black Denim Lit* ("The Line of Fate"), *Digital Americana* ("The Unfortunate Act of Falling"), and the anthology *In Heaven Everything Is Fine: Fiction Inspired by David Lynch* ("First Movement").

Thank you to Steve Gillis, Dan Wickett, Guy Intoci, Michelle Dotter, Michael Seidlinger, and Steven Seighman for bringing this book to life.

Special thanks to William Akin for tackling the first edit of this book, and for teaching me the proper way to use ganache.